# THE DEAD SISTER

## AN ADAM LAPID MYSTERY

JONATHAN DUNSKY

# BOOKS BY JONATHAN DUNSKY

## ADAM LAPID SERIES

Ten Years Gone

The Dead Sister

The Auschwitz Violinist

A Debt of Death

A Deadly Act

The Auschwitz Detective

A Death in Jerusalem

The Unlucky Woman (short story)

## STANDALONE NOVELS

The Payback Girl

*To my sister, Sharon.*

# 1

I knew he was an Arab the moment I saw him. I didn't know why, but I could recognize Germans and Arabs immediately. Perhaps it was because I had killed a good number of each— Arabs during Israel's War of Independence, Germans after the World War in Europe.

This particular Arab was dressed in plain brown pants held up by a slim black belt. His shirt was white, open at the neck, and tucked into his pants. His jacket was dark blue and unbuttoned. He stood in the doorway to Greta's Café and mopped his forehead with a white handkerchief.

Greta's Café was a cozy establishment on Allenby Street in Tel Aviv, a short walking distance from my apartment. It served as a sort of second home and office to me. I ate and drank there every day, and more often than not, prospective clients found me at my table at the rear, playing chess against myself with a board Greta kept for me under the counter.

The Arab put the handkerchief back in his pocket and stepped over to Greta. She was sitting in her regular spot behind the counter, close to the entrance to the café, and reading a newspaper, shaking her head slowly at the news. Greta was a big woman. Tall, wide at the hips and chest, with a fleshy face that had been wrinkled by age and sun, and iron-gray hair arranged in a nest-like halo of curls about her head. The Arab said something to her. I couldn't hear what he was saying, but toward the end of it, Greta cast a quick inquiring glance my way, and I nodded to her.

Greta gestured toward me. The Arab squinted in my direction, nodded his thanks to her, and came over to my table.

Up close I could see he was of medium height and build, but walked with a slight stoop that made him seem shorter than he really was. He wore his black hair longer than most men did, and when he turned his head I could see why. A cigarette-wide pink-white scar ran along his left cheekbone and up to his ear, where it was curtained by his hair. It looked like a bullet had grazed his cheek and mangled his ear some. Or a knife.

Despite the scar, his olive-tone features were delicate, almost feminine. Short and narrow nose, soft brown eyes, rounded chin and jawline. He was clean-shaven. A pair of wire-rim glasses hung on his nose, giving him the air of an intellectual.

"Adam Lapid?"

I nodded, and he said his name was Ahmed Jamalka. I motioned for him to sit. I stuck a cigarette in my mouth, got it going, and offered him the pack. He gave a smile of thanks, but shook his head.

"Those cigarettes aren't for me. I have my own."

From his jacket pocket he drew a thin stack of rolling papers and a small dark-red pouch that, once opened, emitted a strong scent of tobacco. He took one rolling paper and spread a thin layer of tobacco in its center. With quick, dexterous movements, his fingers rolled the paper into an even cylinder, twisted both ends, and tamped them closed. He ran the tip of his tongue over the seam of the cigarette, sealing the paper.

"If you would oblige me with a light," he said, and his voice was as gentle as his features. But it was a gentleness founded in resolve. This was not a man who could be stepped on or over. Not without a fight.

I struck a match and held it out for him. He bent forward to meet flame to cigarette, and I saw that his hair was beginning to thin on top. He looked to be in his early twenties, about ten years younger than I was, much too young to be balding.

He leaned back and we smoked for a while. The scent of his tobacco was fuller and richer than mine.

"What kind of tobacco is that?" I asked.

"It comes from Beirut. In Lebanon. I first encountered it when I was a student there before the war. No other tobacco comes close."

"How do you get it? I thought the borders are closed."

"Officially they are, but no border is ever hermetically closed. My family has some contacts in Lebanon that keep us modestly supplied. Still, I do have to use less tobacco in my cigarettes than I did in the past." He eyed me with a faint smile. "Would you like to try one?"

"It wouldn't feel right, with you having to ration yourself."

"These days, is there anything one doesn't need to ration? Should simple courtesy be postponed to a more prosperous time?"

I nodded agreement with his logic, and he proceeded to roll a cigarette for me. While doing so, he said, "You can consider this a part of your retainer, Mr. Lapid."

I snuffed out my cigarette. "A retainer for what, Mr. Jamalka?"

"For a job I want to hire you to perform." He handed me the cigarette. "Here."

I lit it and took a drag. It was too deep and the tobacco surprisingly strong. I coughed and my eyes watered. Jamalka smiled at me through the haze of smoke our twin cigarettes made between us.

"Good, eh?"

I drew in on the cigarette again, a shallower pull this time. I nodded. "Very good. A new taste, for me at least. The taste of European cigarettes, or American ones, is vastly different. Would you like some coffee to go with it?"

He said that he would, and I asked Greta to bring each of us a cup. We smoked in silence while we waited, gazing at each other through the smoke. He was scrutinizing me more closely than I was him, trying to get the measure of me. He had come here specifically to hire me, but he was hesitant. Whatever task he wanted me to perform, it was of a deeply personal nature. Just revealing it to me might be cause for embarrassment.

It could be anything. He might be blackmailed by someone and could not go to the police. His wife might be having an affair. He might suspect his business partner was stealing from him. But whatever it was, Ahmed Jamalka did not relish sharing it with me.

Greta set the coffee on our table, and Jamalka and I both took a sip. Jamalka nodded at Greta and said, "This is very good. I admit I am surprised."

Greta smiled and thanked him before returning to her chair by the entrance.

He took another sip, seeming to weigh the coffee in his mouth as he contemplated how to tell me what was on his mind.

I said, "There is always tomorrow, Mr. Jamalka."

"What's that?"

"You obviously have a reluctance to talk about whatever brought you here today. Unless it is of an urgent nature, you can always come back another day."

"Do you always tell prospective clients to go away, Mr. Lapid?"

"No. But I'm not that hungry for work, so I don't mind if you do."

He flashed a smile that quickly died, his face turning serious. He gave a small nod of decision, brought out a picture from his inside jacket pocket, and laid it on the table. "This is my sister, Maryam."

I picked up the photo. It was a picture of a young woman, or perhaps a girl on the cusp of becoming a woman. She was slim, black-haired, olive-skinned. She was wearing a white, ankle-length dress that did not cling to the contours of her body, but could not hide her fine figure. At her back was a wall of rough stones. At her feet was a big pot with a wooden spoon sticking out of it. A small dark-furred dog with a white spot on its nose peered up at her from the corner of the picture.

"And here is another." Jamalka handed me another picture.

This one was a close shot. It showed Maryam's face. She had the same eyes as her brother and almost the same nose and mouth. They looked better on her than they did on him.

"She is quite beautiful," I said.

"Yes," he said softly. "And the pictures fail to capture her essence, her vitality, her spirit."

I put both pictures on the table.

"And what do you wish me to do? Is Maryam missing? Do you want me to find her?"

Jamalka shook his head slowly. "That's not it, Mr. Lapid. You see, Maryam is dead. It's her murderer I want you to find."

## 2

I asked, "How did she die? How long ago?"

"Maryam's body was discovered a month ago in Tel Aviv. The nineteenth of September, to be exact. She'd been stabbed. Don't ask me the particulars. The police would not release their reports to me. But I can tell you that he had cut her face up pretty badly. She was no longer beautiful."

"When did you see her?"

"When I made the formal identification at the morgue. I wanted to see the rest of her injuries, but the medical examiner wouldn't let me. He said that he didn't want me to see the autopsy stitches, but I had a feeling her wounds were what he was trying to keep me from seeing."

"Most people wouldn't handle well seeing a loved one dead and exposed like that."

"Well, I didn't get the chance," he said. "Not that it mattered. Seeing her face was bad enough." His cigarette had burned to a stub, and he crushed it out in the ashtray. "The rest you will need to find out for yourself."

"Murder is a matter for the police to investigate," I said.

"It normally is. But not this time."

"What makes Maryam's murder the exception?"

"I do not want the police involved in the matter. Which suits them fine, I should add, as they don't seem to want to be involved either."

"That doesn't seem right. The police here take murder very seriously, Mr. Jamalka."

"Even that of an Arab woman?"

"Even that," I said.

"Well, if they do, they have little to show for it. The detective in charge, Sergeant Yossi Talmon, has been giving me the runaround for weeks. If I had to guess, no progress has been made, and I doubt any would be made."

"And you? Why don't you want the police involved?"

He gazed at me levelly and in a flat tone said, "When the time comes, when the murderer is discovered, I want to take care of him myself, Mr. Lapid. Rather than see him stand trial and, if he's found guilty, spend a few years in prison. I would like to mete out his punishment myself. It's a matter of family pride. It's the way we do things."

I took a last drag off my cigarette, looking at him through the thinning smoke.

"You want to kill him," I said simply.

"Yes. Is that a problem for you?"

"It is against the law. If I do find out who did this, I would be expected to go to the police with what I know."

"But it's not a moral problem?"

No, I thought. It wasn't. I was not averse to killing murderers, especially not the murderers of women. I had done so before, but only when the authorities would or could not deliver justice themselves. But why should I stick my neck out for this man? I didn't know him. I didn't know that I could trust him. And he was asking me to break the law, to be an accessory to murder. I ran my finger around the rim of my cup and looked at him.

"How far does this go, the way you do things? Your vengeance? Is it limited to the murderer, or does it extend to his family?"

He smiled thinly. "I give you my word that no one but the man or men who killed Maryam will be hurt. Does that satisfy you?"

"No," I said. "It does not. I don't run a killing operation here, Mr. Jamalka. If you do hire me and I discover who killed your sister, I intend to hand him over to the police for trial. Take it or leave it."

He stared at me narrow-eyed and tight-jawed for a moment. "And if I won't be satisfied with a jail sentence and decide to kill him nonetheless?"

"That's your business. Not mine. Let me point out, however, that in that case the police will know to come knocking on your door. Your motive will be clear."

"Do you take this position because you think the killer is a Jew?"

"Why would I think that?" I said.

"She was found dead in Tel Aviv. There aren't a lot of Arabs here."

He was right about that. Tel Aviv was a predominately Jewish city. Even after the merger of Tel Aviv with its southern neighbor Jaffa, a port city with a sizable Arab population, into a single municipality earlier that year, Jews were the distinct majority in the joint city.

"The war is over, Mr. Jamalka. For the moment, at least. I don't care who killed your sister or whether he is a Jew or a Muslim or anything else. A murderer is a murderer in my book. I just don't go around killing people if I can help it. I've done too much of that. So make up your mind. Hire me or not. It's your decision."

He lowered his head, thinking it over. At length he said, "Fine. We'll do it your way. It's not like I have much of a choice. I can't do this myself. I needed a permit just to come to Tel Aviv today."

I nodded and told him I would need a retainer to get started. I stated a sum. He didn't haggle. He put the money on the table. I took it and put it in my pocket. We did not shake hands. He finished his coffee. I asked him whether he would like another one, and he said he wouldn't.

I slid the chessboard to the side of the table and took out my notebook and pen. "When was the last time you saw Maryam?"

"Eight months ago."

I raised an eyebrow. "Why so long ago?"

He shifted in his seat. "She…she and my father had a falling out. Maryam had fallen in love with a man, a Christian from a neighboring village. We are Muslims. My father forbade her to see him. She refused to obey him. I begged her to see reason, told her that besides being a non-Muslim, the man had a reputation as a seducer of young women, but she wouldn't listen. Said she would marry this man, leave our faith, and convert to Christianity to be with him."

"What is the name of this man?"

"He's not important. He's not a suspect."

"Why?"

"He's dead."

"How did he die?"

"My older brothers found him." Jamalka's jaw tightened. "He had taken her honor, you see. It was as I had thought. He was not planning to marry her. He simply used her."

"Is that also part of the way you do things?" I asked.

He looked at me for a moment. Then he simply said, "Yes. That is also part of it."

"And Maryam? Had she not brought shame upon your family? Is killing her part of the way you do things as well?"

Color seeped into his cheeks and his scar burned scarlet. He didn't look gentle any longer. Now he looked like a man who could kill you without losing a moment of sleep. "Don't dare judge our ways, Jew. Is it not your way to mourn a family member who has left the faith as if she were dead?"

"The very religious among us may do so," I allowed, "but it is make-believe. No one actually goes out and kills anyone. There is a difference there. Perhaps it is best for you and your family that the police are not pursuing this as hard as they should."

We stared at each other across the table. There was anger in his eyes, the hatred of the defeated. Israel's War of Independence was not long over, and the wounds of the vanquished and those of the victors were far from healed. But along with the hatred and anger, there was also shame. I was right about his culture's acceptance of honor killings, and he knew it. It was a tense moment, and I thought he might get up and leave. But then his shoulders loosened, and he let out a slow exhalation.

"My brothers did not kill Maryam."

"Are you sure about that? You say that they have killed before and that they wouldn't have a moral inhibition against killing your sister."

"I asked them about it directly. They told me they didn't. And I don't think they would hide this from me."

"You were close to your sister," I said.

"Yes."

"Closer than your older brothers were."

"Yes. They are my half brothers. Born from my father's first and second wives. Maryam and I are the only offspring of his third. Our mother died delivering Maryam. She and I were like a small family within the larger family of my father. That is why we were so close."

"Then maybe your brothers lied to you."

He shook his head. "They wouldn't. They would have killed her if they knew where to find her. And had they killed her, they would have boasted about it. Especially to me. You see, they suspect I helped Maryam run away."

"And did you?"

"No. I wish I had, but the truth is I did nothing. She came to me for help, but I turned her away. As for my brothers, I am quite confident they did not kill her. And I must insist that you not speak to them, nor to anyone of my family. No one in my family had any contact with Maryam since she left. Not even me. And no one knows I am here talking to you today."

"That's not the way I generally do things," I said.

"Well, this is how you must do things in this case, or are you going to tell me to take my business elsewhere for the third time?"

I smiled and said, "All right. You're the client. I'll do it your way. If I run into a dead end because of your constraints, I'll let you know, and you'll decide how to proceed. Agreed?"

"Agreed. I'll take that coffee now."

I got us each a fresh cup, and he rolled himself a cigarette, which he lit, and one for me, which I laid aside for later.

I asked him a few more questions and noted the relevant answers in my notebook. Maryam was seventeen when she began the affair with the Christian man—now dead—which led to her expulsion from her father's household. She was eighteen when she died. What her life was like or how she'd sustained herself during the intervening eight months was unknown to her brother.

He talked a great deal about Maryam, showering me with useless information. She liked horses and flowers and had a beautiful singing voice. She baked the best bread in their village and was smart and funny. Up to her late teens she was also quite devout. He cursed the man who had seduced her. He loved his sister a great deal. His heart broke when she ran away from home, and shattered when she was found dead. He also blamed himself for rejecting her when she asked for his help and for not making a greater effort to remain in her life. He had chosen his role as a dutiful son to his father over that of a loving brother to his young sister. And now he was tormented to the point where he came to me, a Jew, for help.

Despite acquiescing to his demand not to speak with his brothers and father, I did get some information regarding them. His father was old, past seventy, and the leader of his clan and village. A strict man who believed in the traditional ways, who thought sons and especially daughters should know their place and obey their elders. There had been five older brothers. One had died during the Arab revolt against the British in 1937. Another had been killed in battle against Jewish forces in 1948. A third had joined a paramilitary group in Lebanon, promising when he left to return triumphant and expel all the Jews from Israel, and had not been heard of since.

"My two remaining brothers and I also fought against you," he told me, pride and defiance edging his voice. "I got this"—he gestured to his scar—"fighting up north. Did you fight in the war, Mr. Lapid?"

"Yes."

"In the north?"

"No. I fought in Jerusalem and in the Negev, for the most part."

"So we didn't fight one another."

Yes, we did, I thought. Whether you and I faced each other across a specific battlefield or not was not important. We were enemies, and perhaps we would be again in the future. None of that mattered to me. A woman was dead and her murderer was out there somewhere. And I had received money to find him. Anything else was extraneous and unimportant.

I looked him over, this gentle-seeming man. Even with the scar on his cheek, he did not look like a soldier. But, I reminded myself, I had met many such men, and many of them turned out to be excellent soldiers. War had the ability to shape men to fit the mold of a fighter.

I asked, "At no point during the eight months since she ran away did Maryam attempt to contact you?"

He shook his head.

"Is it possible that Maryam remained in contact with anyone in your village? One of the women, perhaps?"

"Not that I know. I don't think she did. We're a small village, Mr. Lapid, an extended family in a way. I would have heard something."

I tapped my pen on my notebook, thinking that I wouldn't be able to speak with any of the women either. Their husbands and fathers wouldn't allow it, even if Ahmed Jamalka did.

"Is there anything else you can tell me?" I asked, guessing that there wasn't.

He confirmed my guess with a shake of his head.

I scratched between my eyes. He had given me very little. Next to nothing, really, and his restrictions might hamper my investigation. But that was all right. He had paid for my services; he had the right to give me directions.

We exchanged telephone numbers where we could leave messages to each other, and I said I would give him a progress report in a week, or sooner if I learned something important before that.

I flipped the notebook closed and stared at him. He stared right back at me. I said, "There is a chance that you're wrong, you know. About your brothers, I mean."

He said nothing.

"What happens if, without speaking to your brothers, I discover that they killed your sister?"

He let out a long breath, and his hand went to his scar in what I perceived to be an involuntary motion.

"Then I have made a big mistake coming to you," he said finally, in a voice that was small yet resolute.

There was no more to say. I nodded. "All right, I'll get to it."

He got to his feet, glancing at the chessboard.

"Take the black bishop with the white queen. It's mate in three moves after that."

Then he turned and left the café. I took the cigarette he had rolled for me and sniffed it. Even unlit it had a rich, satisfying scent. I pulled the chessboard closer and moved the white queen as he'd instructed me. For once I played slow, trying to find a way for black to get out of its predicament. Three moves later white won. I smiled. Ahmed Jamalka had left with an oblique parting shot.

# 3

After Ahmed Jamalka had left, I began resetting the chessboard for another game. I played only against myself, and I always played lightning games, with less than a second between moves. It was the only way to play with yourself as the opponent without it becoming boring. When you made moves quickly, the game could shift in all sorts of unpredictable directions. I enjoyed playing like that. It was a great way to exercise the mind without actually thinking about anything.

Greta came over to my table and sat in the chair Jamalka had just vacated. "A new client," she said. "Business is picking up."

"Or maybe society is going down."

"Already? We've only been a country for eighteen months."

"Seventeen months, to be exact," I said with a smile. It was now October 20, 1949, and Israel had been independent since May 1948.

She ran the numbers in her mind. After a second she nodded. "You're right. Seventeen months. Why, that's even worse. You would think it would take us more time than that to screw things up."

I said, "We have three thousand years of experience as a people, maybe that's why." I showed her the rolled cigarette. "He gave me this as a gift."

"That was nice of him." Greta sniffed the lingering smoke in the air. "It smells better than what you usually smoke."

"And tastes better too. But don't get used to it. This is the only one I have. Soon it's back to my usual dreck."

"I'm sorry to hear that. And I'll be sorry to smell it, too. You know, I was looking over at the two of you while you were talking. There was one time I was sure he was about to leap across the table at you, fists first."

I chuckled. "He wanted to. And more than once. And who knows, he might not have used his fists, not if he had a knife in his pocket."

Greta looked horrified. "Don't joke about such things, Adam. Haven't we had enough blood spilled in this country already?"

Enough to fill the Mediterranean, I thought. And we were far from done. Of that, I was sure. But I kept my predictions to myself. Instead I said, "Don't worry. He wouldn't have attacked me. For one thing, he wants me to do something for him. For another, had he attacked me, he would have been thrown in jail. And he needs to be free for at least a while longer."

"Why is that?"

Because he wanted to be ready when I found out who killed his sister, I thought. He couldn't kill him if he himself was locked up.

I said, "Because when I accomplish what he hired me to do, he wants to be able to act on it as soon as possible."

"Do you really think he had a knife on him?"

"Can't say for sure, but I don't think so. He's the sort of man who only carries a weapon when he intends to use it."

"When I saw him enter," Greta said, "I didn't know whether

to be scared or not. At first glance he looks harmless, but that scar..." She gave a shudder.

"Just a few drops of that blood we were talking about. But just because it's ugly does not mean that he hates having it. He said he got it while fighting us in the war. I think it gives him a good deal of pride. Like a medal or a badge of honor."

"You men with your honor," Greta said, shaking her head.

I smiled, but only for a moment, as I recalled what the besmirching of honor could mean for the women in Ahmed Jamalka's culture. And for the men too.

Greta gave me a thoughtful look. "Your face just went two shades darker in the blink of an eye. This isn't a usual job he hired you for, is it?"

"For now I'm not entirely sure what it is. But usual, it isn't. As for the client, you shouldn't be scared of him. He is angry and he doesn't like us Jews very much, but he's reserving his anger for someone other than you or me."

"I hope you're right," she said, "and I feel sorry for that some-one, whoever he may be."

We were silent for a bit, and then she said, "You know, he stopped by me on his way out and paid for the coffee you two drank."

"I saw him hand you money and guessed as much."

"I told him there was no need, that it was taken care of, but he insisted."

"His pride again. He doesn't want to owe a Jew anything. Not even the price of a cup of coffee." I looked at her. "Well, at least you got paid."

"Yes, I suppose that's right. Maybe you should have him over every day."

I first started frequenting Greta's Café in January 1949. It was shortly after I was released from the hospital, where I'd spent a shade over a month recuperating from two bullet wounds I had taken fighting the Egyptian Army in Israel's War of Independence. We became close, Greta and I, especially after I helped her get rid of some self-appointed tough guy who was trying to get her to pay him protection money.

Once he went away, no longer looking or sounding tough, Greta and I came to an understanding. In lieu of payment, I would get to eat and drink at her café for free. I didn't drink or eat much, so I wasn't abusing the privilege, and she felt safer just having me around. So I got my second home, and she got me as a permanent fixture. It was a nice setup.

"I doubt we'll be seeing him anytime soon," I said. "You will have to make do with me, I'm afraid."

Greta let out a long, laborious sigh. "Well, that's all right. As a Jew, I'm used to making do with what little is available."

We exchanged smiles. She said I would have to excuse her and went to serve coffee to a florid-faced customer who was beckoning her from the other side of the room.

I took the cigarette Ahmed Jamalka had given me, fired it up, and inhaled the rich smoke deep into my mouth and chest. I held the smoke in as long as I could before I vented it out in a thick, aromatic stream of black and gray. I set up the chess pieces on the board and swiveled it around so that I was now facing white. One more quick game to go along with this fine cigarette, and then I'd start working on finding out who had killed Maryam Jamalka.

# 4

I exited Greta's and turned south on Allenby. I smoked a cigarette as I walked, and wished I hadn't. The cheap tobacco erased all traces of the quality cigarette Ahmed Jamalka had given me.

I crossed Rothschild Boulevard and took a right to Yehuda Halevi Street. I followed the road west. I had finished my smoke by the time I got to the three-story building that stood at number 6. The blue and white flag of Israel was lazily blowing in the faint breeze on its roof, and a wide rectangular sign over the entrance proclaimed the building to be a police station of the Tel Aviv district.

I climbed the stairs to the second floor, took a right past some open offices, and found the one occupied by Reuben Tzanani. He was inside, with his back to me, arranging files and folders in a gray metal filing cabinet.

I stood in the doorway, watching him for a moment. Reuben was a short man, five foot four with shoes on, with a frame that was slight and narrow. His unimpressive physique gave a false impression. Reuben was as tough as they come, and me being alive was testament to that.

The previous October, he and I fought side by side against the Egyptian Army during Operation Yoav in the south of Israel. It was a series of harsh and bitter battles and skirmishes, and during one of them, I'd taken two bullets to the torso. Despite my being nearly a foot taller and forty pounds heavier, Reuben had hoisted me on his back and carried me for over a kilometer to the rear, where I'd received the emergency care that kept me from dying that day.

For what he'd done, Reuben received a small citation and a nickname. In our unit he became known as "Ant" for his ability to carry more than his body weight for long distances.

For my injury, and for certain actions I had taken earlier in that battle, I was lauded as a war hero, awarded a medal, and given the rank of sergeant. Reuben was far more deserving of accolades and promotions than I, but it never seemed to bother him any.

Finished with his files, he pushed the drawer closed, grimacing when it squeaked.

"You should oil that," I said. "Use some of the oil from all the Yemenite food you eat. It might taste better."

He turned and grinned at me.

Reuben had a grin so wide it seemed on the verge of splitting his face in two. It lit up a room, or a military encampment, better than a lamp or a blazing campfire. His features were small and well-shaped. A short nose, rounded cheeks, a tall, smooth forehead. His head was crowned with tight, black curls.

"Better than the dry food you Hungarians eat," he said, taking his chair. "That's why you need to drink so much and why you look so pale."

I smiled and sat across from him.

This exchange of jabs and insults regarding the food each of us had grown up with was something we had been doing since shortly after we met. Reuben took great pride in Yemenite food and found it humorous that I had trouble handling some of the spicier dishes he enjoyed. For my part, my praise for Hungarian cuisine was feigned. I had to admit that there was little contest. Yemenite food was far superior to Hungarian.

I asked him how his wife, Gila, and his children were, and he beamed when he spoke of them. He had four children and they were all fine and healthy. He told me a little about each, and from the sound of it, he wouldn't have minded having a fifth in the near future. We talked a little about how things were slowly improving now that the war was officially over, and he spoke with great emotion about the thousands of Yemenite Jews that were arriving by the week to Israel. Apparently, there were many distant relatives of his among them.

Finally, we ran out of mundane things to talk about, and he asked what brought me to his office.

"A murder case."

Reuben's eyebrows shot up. "A murder case? Who's the victim?"

"A young woman. The name is Maryam Jamalka."

"I don't think I ever heard the name," Reuben said. "Was she killed in Tel Aviv?"

"Yes."

"When?"

"Her body was discovered on the nineteenth of September. She was stabbed. I understand it was quite brutal."

Reuben's brow furrowed. "That's odd," he said softly. He looked perplexed. I could see why. Tel Aviv did not have many murders, especially brutal ones. A desk policeman like Reuben, one who spent most of his workday in the station, in the hub of police operations, should have heard something about it.

"Are you sure about this, Adam?"

"Unless my client was lying to me, which I don't think he was. Or unless he's a lunatic, which I don't think he is, either. Yes, I'm sure."

"Okay. I can ask around." He wrote down Maryam Jamalka's name and the date on which her body was discovered on a scrap of paper. "What do you need to know?"

"Everything," I said. "The best thing would be to see the investigation report or talk to the detective in charge. His name is Yossi Talmon. Do you know him?"

Reuben nodded. "Not closely. He has a solid reputation, though. Long years of experience, a good investigator. I'll talk to him and see if he's willing to share any information. But if this is an open case, he may not be willing to share much. Especially if your client is a possible suspect. Is he?"

I shook my head slowly. "I doubt it. Guilty men generally don't hire private detectives to investigate the murders they committed."

"Good point. Well, I'll give it a try, Adam, and hope for the best. I should have an answer by tomorrow. Call me at noon or so?"

"I will. Thank you," I said.

We talked for a few minutes more, and he invited me over for the Sabbath meal that Friday evening. I begged off, and he nodded as if expecting it. Which he was justified in doing, as he often invited me, and I nearly always declined.

I exited the police station shortly before five thirty and headed north on Allenby. A faint easterly breeze was blowing, and the air held a pleasant chill. I bought an orange-flavored soda from a street vendor and continued walking till I got to Magen David Square. I had a few hours to burn, so I purchased a bunch of newspapers, sat at a bench, and read them through.

In the United Nations Security Council, Egypt was promoting a proposal for the demilitarization of Jerusalem. In

Haifa, during a brawl in a café, an Arab pulled out a gun and shot a soldier in the leg. The Arab was still at large. The Kingdom of Transjordan was said to look favorably on the possibility of cooperating with Israel on various development projects in the Jordan Valley. Two hundred and forty Romanian Jews were stuck in the port of Constanta, awaiting approval from the Romanian government to board a ship that would take them to Israel. The Jews were said to be without food and shelter. Following the USSR, Poland had recognized the German Democratic Republic. In Guatemala, over a thousand people died due to heavy rains and flooding.

I left the newspapers on the bench and went home to get ready for what I had to do later that night.

# 5

I lived on Hamaccabi Street, in a third-floor, one-bedroom apartment. It was simply and functionally furnished. I had a bed, a nightstand topped by a lamp, a dining table, a couple of straight-backed wooden chairs, and a closet. The walls were blank, no pictures, paintings, or ornamentation of any kind. The kitchen was small and the bathroom even smaller. There was a balcony that could fit two people, if they were trim.

Upon entering my apartment, I removed my jacket, threw it on the dining table, and left my shoes by the door. I flicked on the light and drew all the shutters closed across the window and sliding door to the balcony.

In the closet, beneath a false bottom I had constructed for the purpose, I had hidden a box. It was a simple box made of oak, with a clasp at its center. I scratched the number tattooed on my forearm, then took out the box, carried it with me to my bed, and lifted the lid.

Inside the box I had stashed several souvenirs of the time I had spent in Germany between the day I was liberated by American soldiers at Buchenwald and September 1947, when I came to Tel Aviv. During that time, I had hunted down and executed a number of Nazi officers and officials, men who were part of the murder machine that had claimed the lives of my mother and sisters, of my wife and daughters, and of so many others.

Among the mementos I kept in the box was a Luger pistol. I had taken it from an SS officer I'd killed in Hamburg. I also had two magazines for the pistol and a number of loose shells. I kept the pistol clean and loaded at all times, ready for use. Also in the box was a pearl-handled switchblade hunting knife. The knife had been taken from another officer I'd killed, this one in Munich, and had a swastika stamped near the bottom of its handle.

I couldn't say why I kept this particular knife or the Luger pistol. It wasn't merely for protection. I could have found replacements for either of them. In fact, having the knife, marked as it was by the symbol of the Third Reich, might have exposed me to some inconvenient questions. But I liked having these two items, along with my other souvenirs. I liked having them near. I liked looking at them. I liked touching them. And, if the occasion merited it, I liked using them as well.

I removed the knife and set it on the bed beside me. I left the other items where they lay and returned the box to its hiding place in the closet. I made myself some dinner—vegetables, bread, a little sausage, two cups of coffee. I rinsed the dishes, dried them, and returned them to the cupboard above the sink where I kept the three plates and four glasses I owned. I spent the next two hours reading a Western with a rough-faced cowboy on the cover. Then I put my jacket back on, slipped the knife in the right-hand pocket, and left the apartment.

On the street, I paused to get a cigarette going. I saw people standing on their balconies, leaning on railings, talking or smoking or just enjoying the cool night air. A few waved to me or nodded a silent greeting. I nodded back as I made my way to the corner and from there to the bus station on King George Street. I waited for ten minutes then got on a half-full bus with a racketing engine. At the front of the bus, an old woman sat with a red ball of wool, knitting at a furious pace. I wondered how she could make out what she was doing with the scant light offered by the streetlights and the passing illumination from cafés and apartments. The bus trundled its way south, disgorging people as it went. I got off near the eastern tip of Shalma Road a little before ten and started west.

I walked along Shalma Road all the way to Hashaon Square, about one hundred meters east of the coastline. In the middle of the square stood a clock tower that had been built to celebrate the reign of an Ottoman sultan. Now the sultans were gone, along with the empire they once ruled, but the clock at the tower's tip still marked the time.

I took a left to Yefet Street and followed it south. Yefet Street, and some of the narrow streets that branched from it, changed character at nightfall. During the day, they were home to small shops and assorted merchants. At night, after the shopkeepers had locked their storefronts and gone home, a variety of less savory institutions opened for business. Among them were nightclubs in which one could dance and drink till the early hours, gambling joints, and whorehouses. It was a poor neighborhood, filled with people who did not have much and some that had close to nothing. And it was rife with crime, which was why I had brought the knife along.

I stepped into a nightclub from which soft undulating music emanated. The inside was dark and hazy, filled with pungent cigarette smoke and the scent of spilled alcohol, sweat, and cheap perfume. The ceiling was high, and pipes ran along it every which way. A bar stretched along the left wall, and two dozen or so one-legged tables were scattered about the rest of the space. At the far end stood a small stage for musicians. It was a weeknight, but half the tables were occupied, and a band was playing. The band consisted of a mandolin player, a violinist, a darbuka percussionist, and a singer. The musicians looked Moroccan, or perhaps Egyptian Jews, and each was highly proficient in his instrument. The singer had dark skin like bitter chocolate and the tall, scrawny build of a lamppost.

I looked around, but the man I was there to see wasn't present. I checked my watch. It was ten thirty-five. He said he would be there before eleven o'clock. It looked like I was going to have to wait.

A burly man with receding hair and a thick black mustache worked the bar. He gave me a suspicious look when I approached. I was expecting it—I was the only Ashkenazi Jew present, the rest were Mizrahi Jews. The music playing in this club originated in North African countries—Morocco, Tunisia, Egypt—and was not the usual fare of Ashkenazi Jews. If I had to bet on it, I was the only Ashkenazi patron they'd had since they opened their doors. I ordered a beer. The bartender made no move to get me one. Perhaps he thought I was a policeman, there to hassle them. It was quite possible there was a card or dice game in some back room and the bartender was concerned I might be there to bust it. If he did, he was a fool, for no policeman in his right mind would raid a club by himself. Another possibility was he thought I was there to put the squeeze on them. Quite a few policemen supplemented their income that way. There was no point in finding out what was bothering him. I clanged some coins on the bar. "I'm not here to make trouble," I said. "Just want to enjoy the music for a while. Get me a beer, please."

He pressed his lips for a moment, then, wordlessly, got a tall glass and poured beer into it. He didn't tilt the glass, so the head accumulated, filling up half the glass. I didn't complain. Getting into a fight over cheap beer wasn't what I was there for.

I carried my glass to a vacant table, dropped into a chair, took a sip of the beer, and took in the band. The singer alternated between Hebrew and Arabic and was fluent in both. His voice was high and clear, and he delivered the lyrics in loopy ululations that curled around the room like flitting butterflies. The singer's skill, the rapid finger play across mandolin strings, and the lively beat of the percussionist gave an air of unbridled festivity, and there was an invitation in those songs, an exhortation to be happy, even when one's fortunes indicated a different emotion was in order.

The melodies were new to me, and when the song was in Arabic, the lyrics incomprehensible. Yet I found myself tapping the toe of my shoe to the beat of the music. It spoke to a deeper level than understanding and tugged at a basic rhythm within my body and mind. I wished I had arrived there earlier in the evening so I could have enjoyed more of the set.

Some of the patrons were slipping me suspicious looks similar to that given me by the bartender. I didn't pay them much mind, kept nursing my beer, and periodically checked my watch.

Shortly after eleven I saw Charlie Buzaglo enter the bar, a slim dark-haired girl in a tight-fitting black dress on his arm. He went to the bar, shook hands with the bartender, and waited while the latter poured him two tall glasses of a clear liquid. He gave one to the girl, took one for himself, and surveyed the club. It was dark, and apparently he didn't see me, because he led the girl to a table. They sat close together, his arm around her shoulders.

I rose, taking my near-empty glass with me, and went to his table.

"Hello, Charlie," I said.

He squinted up at me. "There you are. I've been waiting for you."

"Hardly," I said. "I've been here for twenty minutes."

28

"Well, anyway, it's good that you're here. We need to talk, you and I." He took his arm off the pretty girl, who up close looked not a day older than sixteen, and motioned at a vacant chair. I sat, looked at the girl, then back at Charlie. I raised an eyebrow. What we had to talk about was best discussed without an audience.

He nodded once, turned to the girl and said, "Revital, go sit at the bar for a while. I need to talk to Adam in private."

Revital pouted and didn't move. He waved his hand in a shooing motion.

"Go on now. It will only take a few minutes. Then I am all yours for the rest of the night."

She rose with an irritated sigh and strutted to the bar. Charlie watched her with keen eyes until she took a stool, lighting a long cigarette with a match provided by the bartender.

"She is something, isn't she?" he said, still looking at her.

"She's a little young, wouldn't you say?"

He turned to me and smiled. "She's old enough. Trust me on that."

I didn't smile back. I didn't like men who had romances with young girls. I didn't like Charlie Buzaglo. But I had done a job for him, and he had only paid a quarter of the total sum we'd agreed on when he hired me. I was there to collect the rest of it.

"You found your merchandise?" I asked.

Buzaglo's smile faded, and he gave me a long probing look. He was a wiry man, five foot seven in height, with a long, light-brown face topped by black hair that had been combed back and slicked with oil. His nose and chin were sharp and narrow, his mouth small and pinched. He looked like a pampered rat. His close-set eyes were narrow slits as he scrutinized me.

"Everything but Mordecai. He seems to have vanished into thin air."

Buzaglo was a smuggler who had been importing a variety of

goods—food, alcohol, clothes, radios—that were rationed or hard to come by in Israel. He'd hired me a few weeks before, after one of his shipments arrived minus half its intended contents. Missing along with the goods was Mordecai Ohayon, one of Buzaglo's employees. Buzaglo had asked me to find the merchandise, hopefully before it got sold off on the black market, and to locate Ohayon as well.

I'd conducted a quick investigation, which led me to a small warehouse in the town of Herzliya, a few kilometers north of Tel Aviv. On a cot at the back of the warehouse I came across an unshaven and unkempt Mordecai Ohayon. He was asleep, with the hilt of a butcher knife peeking from beneath his thin pillow. When I woke him up, he nearly fainted. He bawled his heart out, begging me not to hurt him. He was sure I'd been sent to beat him to a pulp, if not worse. He never even went for the knife.

I quickly persuaded him that if he wanted to stay in one piece for much longer, running away was his best bet. He tried to take a few whiskey bottles with him as he left, but I wouldn't have it. I was not about to hand him over to Charlie Buzaglo, but I was not going to help him steal from my client either. I told Ohayon he should be happy to get away with all his bones unbroken and all his teeth in his mouth. He left empty-handed. I hoped, for his sake, that he went someplace far away.

Now, Charlie Buzaglo was dissatisfied with me for not delivering to his hands the man who stole from him.

"So you didn't get Mordecai," I said. "But at least the merchandise was all there. That's where you make your money from. So what's the problem?"

"It was all there. But I can't have people robbing from me and getting away with it unpunished."

"Apparently the man can't show his face in public. Isn't that punishment enough?"

"Perhaps," Buzaglo said. "But not quite what I had in mind."

Which was exactly why I didn't hand Ohayon over to him. I was no longer a policeman, and petty crime like a little smuggling did not interest me all that much. God knew, the black market had its uses. Without it, you couldn't get much proper food in Israel. If I had to guess, most of the population bought some items that were restricted. But what would happen to Ohayon if I handed him to Buzaglo was not like buying a little extra butter or meat. It would involve a good deal of violence and pain. I was not about to have that on my conscience. I reserved violent punishment for violent people and murderers, not petty thieves who stole from each other.

"Where do you suppose he is?" Buzaglo asked.

Cyprus, I hoped, for Ohayon's sake. Or maybe somewhere in Europe. I had no idea if he had the money for such a trip. If he was still in Israel, I hoped he was staying low and far away from Tel Aviv.

I said, "He could be anywhere. Out of the country, even."

"This presents us with a problem."

"A problem?"

"Yes. I hired you to find my property and Mordecai. But you haven't found Mordecai. And you're not going to find him, are you?"

I shook my head. "I'm done with this job."

He raised an eyebrow at the disgusted tone of my voice. Truth was, I regretted taking the job in the first place. Working for the likes of Charlie Buzaglo was not how I wanted to spend my time.

Charlie said, "So I'm asking myself why I should be paying you anything."

"Because I got you your goods back," I said.

"Yes. But that wasn't the whole job. I paid you to do two things, and you only did one. You didn't do what I hired you to. You should get nothing from me."

31

I looked at him, with his open-to-mid-chest black shirt and the thin gold-plated bracelet dangling from his wrist. He was a low-life criminal, and I felt dirty just sitting at the same table with him. In a way, it was my fault for taking the job in the first place. I now wished I'd let Mordecai Ohayon take those bottles with him.

"In fact," Buzaglo was saying, "I want you to give back the money I gave you as a retainer."

I raised an eyebrow, thinking he was joking. There wasn't a trace of a smile on his face. Now I understood why he had told me to come to this nightclub in Jaffa to get the rest of my money. He was a regular here, and I was the outsider. If I started anything, there would be five men on me in seconds.

I pushed my chair back and got to my feet. "I don't want your money. Nothing you pay me will make being in your presence worthwhile. But I'm not giving you a single lira back. What you paid me will cover my work in getting you your goods back."

His mouth tightened and his eyes flashed malevolently. For a moment I thought he was going to jump me, and I got ready to punch him in the face and then run for the door. But he stayed in his seat, his ratlike eyes glaring at me. He didn't even respond to my insults.

He slouched back in his chair and waved a hand dismissively at me. "All right," he said. "Go. Get out of here."

I didn't need to be told twice. I put my hand in my pocket, over the knife, and walked quickly to the door. I could feel eyes on me, escorting me on my way, making sure I really left.

# 6

I pushed the door of the club open and stepped outside. It swung shut behind me with a bang, muffling the sound of the band within. Only when I drew my first breath back on the sidewalk did I realize how smoky the nightclub had been. I coughed once to clear my throat, wishing I had some water with me. I took my hand out of my pocket and unclenched the other one. I had unconsciously made a fist with it.

The street was dark and deathly quiet, with less than half the streetlights casting desultory cones of hazy yellow illumination on the dirty pavement below. No lights showed from the windows of the apartments along both sides of the street. The inhabitants had settled in for the night. The only cars in sight were parked. The sidewalks were empty and thick with fathomless shadows.

I started walking away from the bar, and before I made it to the corner, the sound of the music got louder for a second or two, then diminished again. Someone had come out of the bar a minute or so after I did. I turned the corner, focusing my ears on the street behind me, trying to filter out all other sounds.

The city was never silent. There were always the sounds of

vehicles, even at night, even when the street you were walking on was empty. There was the hum of streetlights, the burble of a radio playing melancholy night music, the hooting and squawking of nocturnal birds, the scrabbling of rats scouting for their dinner in inadequately closed trash cans. Still, as I walked that dark Jaffa street, I could make out the light thud of footsteps behind me. One or perhaps two sets of feet. Not running but walking at a brisk pace, faster than I was.

I crossed the street, so what had been to the back of me was now to the right, and I allowed myself a quick glance rightward, as if making sure that no car was coming my way. I spotted two shadows fifty meters or so behind me. They moved and then abruptly stopped, trying to avoid being detected. That was a mistake because it answered the question that was running through my mind—were these men after me?

One of the shadows was tall and thick, the other shorter and narrower. It seemed that Charlie Buzaglo was not about to let me walk away with the retainer he'd paid me. He was coming to get it, or whatever there was in my pockets, and had some goon along with him. I cursed myself for my stupidity in agreeing to come to that bar at night without my Luger. But at least I'd brought the knife. I wasn't a total fool.

A warm tingle swept through my torso and arms. There was some part of me that welcomed the coming fight. For a fight was coming. I wasn't about to run. I was going to face them, and I was going to do it alone. There were no police cruising these streets, and calling for help would be pointless and even counter-productive. The residents of these streets were unlikely to come to my assistance, and I would be advertising to my pursuers that I was aware of their pursuit. Facing two men was not my idea of good odds. But at least they weren't expecting me to have the knife, and they didn't know that I knew they were coming after me. If I could surprise them, I would have a good chance of taking them both down.

I took a left and followed it with a quick right. I kept my pace even, the walk of an oblivious quarry, just taking in the night air, allowing the two men on my tail to slowly narrow the distance between us. I lost track of what street I was on—the signage was bad and I did not know this part of the city very well. A plan was formulating in my mind, but I needed the right place to put it into action. And the right timing. I kept my ears open, trying to gauge the distance of the two men at my back. The hair on the nape of my neck was prickling, and I was suddenly cold and wondering whether one of them had a gun. Could he be pointing it at my back that very second?

I decided that was unlikely. They would have rushed me if they had a gun. They could have shot me dead already.

Up ahead I saw a turn into a narrow cross street no wider than an alleyway. It was dimly lit along its middle, but both sides were pitch black, the kind of darkness that swallows all light and all hope of light as well. It was so dark that, a meter into the alley, you couldn't make out the walls on either side. I gingerly stepped into the alley, the stink of garbage and urine clogging my nostrils. Fifteen meters ahead, the light from a connecting street could be seen. It was as good a place as any to make my stand. I shifted toward the wall to my right, flattened my back against it, and took out the knife, placing my finger on the spring button. My heart was pounding in my ears, and I imagined I could hear my breath as loud as a storm wind. My forehead was drenched in sweat and droplets hung in my eyebrows, some sliding down my cheeks in slick, tear-wide lines. Despite the stench, I took deep, slow, quiet breaths through my nose and tried to calm myself down. They had not been far behind me by that time. Twenty-five meters or less. Soon.

Then I saw them, one tall and one medium in height, at the

mouth of the alley, their frames backlit by the streetlights. The big one was carrying something in his hand. A knife? A billy club?

They moved into the mouth of the alley close together, walking quickly, not seeing me, thinking that I had made it to the street at the far end. I lunged at them, and inadvertently knocked over a metal trashcan that stood blanketed by the darkness. One of them shouted something, and they both turned to me. I'd intended to take the big guy out first with a kick to his kneecap. Instead, my foot glanced off his shin. He yelped in pain but did not go down. He swung the club at me. I lurched back, but its tip swiped my sternum. A burst of pain spread through my torso. My breath caught in my throat and I almost dropped the knife.

He started toward me again, the club raised over his head. He was as tall as I was, and looked bigger across the shoulders and chest. A downward blow on the head from that club would knock me to the ground, if not kill me outright. He was closer now, and I could hear him breathing heavily. The club reached its zenith and started its descent toward my skull.

Charlie Buzaglo saved me. Hurling curses at me, he stepped forward into the path of his accomplice, who had to check his swing. Charlie was now between us, and I took full advantage. I dodged the wild fist he swung at me and punched him in the stomach with my right hand, the folded knife in my fist adding force to the blow. Breath whooshed out of him with a grunt, and Buzaglo folded toward me. I used my shoulder to push him into his accomplice, who, in the rage of battle, simply flung his boss aside to the dirty ground. Buzaglo crashed on top of something wooden and let out a girlish cry of pain.

The big man came at me fast and hard. I stepped back, catching my breath, and caught the side movement of the club aiming at my jaw. I ducked and felt the rush of air on my scalp. I clicked the knife open and stepped closer to my opponent.

If he'd heard the mechanism springing into action, he made no move to escape it. Perhaps he was in that drunken state of battle that turned cowards into brave men and smart men into stupid automatons. Or maybe he just didn't recognize the sound, though most criminals of his kind would.

Or maybe he was smarter than I thought, because he almost knocked me down with the left fist he had waiting for me.

It came hard and straight, like he sensed where I was going and was welcoming my approach. I shifted to the side at the last instant, and the blow got me on the left shoulder instead of my head. It was a good thing I'm right-handed, or the knife would have clattered to the floor. A spasm of pain rushed all the way down to my fingertips, and I let out a low moan. I swiped wildly at his arm with the knife. Warm blood sprayed on my hand, and he shrieked.

He was raging now, out of control with pain and fury. I stepped quickly to the side and back, remembering the club, and when it came, I easily dodged it. My hand was sticky with his blood. I knew I should finish him soon before Buzaglo rejoined the fight, but I didn't want to kill him. I wasn't sure he deserved it.

My eyes had adjusted to the murk, and I could see him well enough to aim. I set myself right and swung from my hips. This time my kick connected. It took his right knee out from under him. He fell in a big heap, and I heard the club stutter away on the dark-engulfed pavement. He was moaning continuously now, bleeding from one arm, with one knee out of commission. For a second I wondered how much he'd been paid by Buzaglo to come after me. I suppressed the thought for now. I wasn't done with either of them yet.

I turned toward where Buzaglo had fallen. He was on his hands and knees now, trying to get to his feet. I planted my foot hard in his stomach and he crumpled like a house in an aerial bombardment. I kicked him in the ribs and heard something crunch, and he whimpered in pain.

"Move and I'll break another one," I said. He stayed still.

I went back to the big guy. His breath quickened as I neared him. He was panting, sure I was there to inflict more pain. The scent of his fear and the coppery odor of blood brought back unwelcome memories of other times I had encountered those smells. I gritted my teeth, shoving the encroaching memories down to the depths of my mind. I had no use for them. Now, or ever.

"I'm going to drag you into the light," I told the big man. "See how bad the cut is. If you try anything, I'll slice you open."

He didn't answer. I grabbed him under the arms and dragged him. He groaned a little, whether due to his knee or his arm, I couldn't say.

When he was in the light, I crouched beside him, my dripping red knife clearly visible.

"What's your name?"

"Rafi," he said. His face was red from exertion and pain and fear.

"What were you going to do to me, Rafi?" I asked him, and when he looked at me uncomprehendingly, I clarified, "Kill me, break some bones, take off some fingers, what?"

He had a big, circular face, with flat, wide, unrefined features. He hadn't shaved for a week or so, and the low stubble on his cheeks was damp with the sweat of the fight and his injuries.

"Just break some bones," he said in a low, frightful voice.

"Sure about that?" I asked.

"Yes. I swear."

I was looking at his eyes as we spoke, searching for the lie. I didn't see it. His eyes stayed on mine the whole time. Wide and brimming with fear, but unwavering.

"All right," I said. "Don't move."

I went through his pockets. If I'd found a knife on him, I didn't know what I would have done to him. But other than some money, cigarettes, a lighter, and a folded picture of a semi-naked brunette, there was nothing.

"Show me your arm," I said.

He held it up with a grimace. It was bleeding fast. He wasn't going to die in the next few minutes, but it was not good, nonetheless. I took hold of his shirt with my left hand, and he flinched when he saw the knife in my right coming closer.

"Relax," I said. "Don't move."

I cut his bloody sleeve away and tossed it aside. I did the same with the clean sleeve and turned it into a makeshift bandage. I wrapped it around his wound and knotted it tight. I looked at it for a moment. Blood was coming out, but very slowly.

"You're going to need to get that stitched," I said, "but you'll live."

He blinked at me questioningly, hope dawning in his eyes.

I said, "If you ever come after me again, I will gut you and let you bleed out. Do you understand me, Rafi?"

He swallowed and nodded, licking his fat bottom lip.

"Can you walk?"

"I think so," he muttered.

I helped him to his feet, and he steadied himself on the side of a building.

"What about Charlie?" he asked.

"Don't worry about him. Worry about me changing my mind."

Fear flashed in his eyes. I think he was about to thank me. Fortunately, he resisted the urge. He turned around and hobbled away.

I walked back into the alleyway. Charlie Buzaglo had turned on his back, and his breath was rasping in and out of his chest like steam in a clogged pipe.

I dragged him out into the light and got down on one knee beside him, showing him the knife. Up close, the stink of his cologne was almost thick enough to gag on. I lifted the hem of his shirt and wiped as much blood as I could off my hand on it.

"I let your friend go," I said. "Now what am I supposed to do with you?"

His eyes bulged so far they looked ready to pop out of their sockets. His mouth fell open. His rat brain was searching for words, but none came. Finally, he said, gasping, "My wallet. Left pocket."

I took his wallet out. It was chock-full of bills. I fanned them in my hand.

I frowned at him. "You have all this on you and you wouldn't pay me?"

He tried shrugging, but the movement shifted his rib cage and he moaned. I had probably broken one or two ribs when I kicked him.

"Go ahead," he said. "Take it all."

I looked at him and shook my head slowly. His eyes turned to saucers with dread.

"Take it. It's yours. Let me go and I'll give you more. Okay?"

I shook my head again and counted out a sum equal to the retainer he'd given me when he hired me. I folded the bills and stuck them in my pocket. The rest I stuffed back in his wallet and placed it on his stomach.

"I did half the work, so I should get half the pay," I said. "I don't want any more of your money."

He just looked at me. He didn't understand me. That was all right. If he did, it would have meant I was doing something wrong.

"So that settles what you owe me for my work. But there is the matter of you trying to break some of my bones."

He started shaking his head, but I held up a hand. It was my right hand, and the sight of the knife and the smeared blood made him draw a sharp intake of breath.

"Don't waste my time. Your friend and I had a talk." When his gaze went over my shoulder, I added, "He's gone to take care of his wounds. We're all alone."

He kept quiet, which was smart. A part of me was itching to beat him up some more. I took a deep calming breath.

"The only smart thing you did, Charlie, was that you didn't come to kill me. You see, I don't like to kill people. I only kill those I have to. And I'm thinking that maybe I don't have to kill you. If you came to kill me, then it would be different. But you didn't, so you get to wake up tomorrow with sore ribs and nothing more. But if you ever come after me again, I will kill you. Is that clear?"

He nodded, his eyes wide with disbelief. He couldn't believe I was letting him go so easy, and without even emptying his wallet.

I held out my left hand to him. He cringed, thinking I was about to strike him. He looked at my hand for a moment before taking it gingerly. I jerked him to his feet and got a sick pleasure when he groaned and grimaced in pain.

We stood looking at each other for thirty seconds or so. Then he looked at his feet, turned and walked quickly away. I stood watching until he disappeared around a corner. I folded the knife and held it in my hand all the way home. When I got to my apartment, I washed my knife and then washed myself. I got into bed and closed my eyes. I knew the nightmares that usually haunted my sleep would not torment me that night. I always slept well at the end of bloody days.

# 7

The next day was Friday. I got up early, restless and impatient. After eating a quick breakfast of bread and margarine and coffee with powdered milk, I went to the corner and entered Levinson Drugstore.

Like the vast majority of people in Israel, I did not have a telephone in my apartment. A home telephone was considered a luxury; the only people who had them were doctors, army officers, politicians, and government officials. There were two such men on Hamaccabi Street, but neither offered the use of his phone to his neighbors. The only phone available to the public was in Levinson Drugstore on the corner of Hamaccabi and King George.

The phone was attached to a meter that calculated what you owed for the call. Each call was limited to fifteen minutes at the most, so as not to create a long line of impatient neighbors. The time limit was maintained with polite but implacable strictness by Mrs. Levinson, who ran the store with her husband.

Luckily, I only had to wait for three minutes for the telephone. I called Reuben.

"Tell me you have something for me," I said.

"Good morning, Adam," he said. "I do indeed. I spoke with Sergeant Talmon, and he has agreed to meet with you."

"When and where?"

"At nine thirty tomorrow night at a café in Holon." Reuben gave me the name of the café and the address.

"Why Holon? Does Talmon live there?"

"I was asking myself the same question, but as far as I know, he lives in Tel Aviv. I have no idea why he would drag you and himself to Holon at such an hour."

I did, but I said nothing.

Reuben went on, "It wasn't easy to persuade him to talk to you, Adam. At first he didn't want to hear of it and was quite brusque when I told him what case you were interested in."

"Maybe he doesn't like the idea of civilians being involved in police matters."

"Maybe, but I think there was something else there. When I first mentioned the name Maryam Jamalka, Talmon got quite upset. He asked who told me about her, and for a moment I considered not giving him your name."

"And in the end?"

"I talked to him some more, and he suddenly changed his tune and said I could arrange the meeting."

"Good. You did good, Reuben. Thank you."

"Just a second, Adam. Talmon was acting very strange. He made me swear not to tell anyone but you about our talk and his agreeing to see you. And he also told me I must not speak to anyone else in the department about the case."

"Did he give a reason for all this secrecy?"

"No. I asked him, and he told me it was none of my business. It's the first time in my career that such a thing has happened."

"I see," I said, though in truth, I was not sure that I did. Since when was a murder case treated like a military secret?

"You must also keep this to yourself, Adam. At least until you meet with him and see what's gotten him all upset."

"I'll tell no one, Reuben."

"I wouldn't want to be caught in the middle of some departmental power struggle or whatever the hell this is."

"No one will know you're involved. Not from my lips, they won't."

He let out a breath of relief, and I cursed myself for involving him in this case. Reuben had saved my life. I would have gladly given my life to save his. I wanted no harm to come to him. There was something fishy going on with this case, and I had no clue what it was. I needed to make sure Reuben would not be harmed by my actions.

"I have to get off the phone, Reuben. Don't worry. Your part in this is over. I'll meet Talmon and see what's going on. I'm sure none of it will ever get to you."

"I hope you're right, Adam."

"Sure I am. Thanks for all your help, Reuben. Forget about this whole thing, and we'll talk soon."

I hung up, went out to the street, and leaned against a stone fence with a cigarette burning between two fingers. I ran my mind over my conversation with Reuben and added Ahmed Jamalka's impressions of the investigation the police were conducting. What it added up to was that there was a murder about which the police were doing very little, and it was shrouded in such secrecy that not even police officers were supposed to know about it. I couldn't figure out a reason for these two facts and gave up trying once my cigarette had burned its way to half an inch from my fingers. I would know tomorrow, I hoped. When I met with Sergeant Yossi Talmon.

# 8

Holon was a city that, like Tel Aviv, had risen out of the dunes of the coastal plain of Israel. But unlike its sister to the north, Holon did not develop into a culture and nightlife center, but remained a bedroom community peopled by hardworking men and women of low to moderate income. The residents of Holon mostly worked as day laborers in construction projects throughout the Tel Aviv district, or they held various blue-collar jobs in small workshops and factories in the area. Many were employed in the local textile factory. Holon's buildings showed none of the flare of the Bauhaus architecture of Tel Aviv. They eschewed artistry in favor of functionality. Consequently, the streets of Holon were lined with tenements of gray-white stone with a rough exterior and a modest, utilitarian interior.

I got off the bus at the Holon terminal and made my way west. Men in undershirts and women in plain dresses stood smoking on open balconies. Screeching cats fought turf wars over garbage cans. Open windows let out the sounds of radios and family squabbles, along with a confusing mix of cooking scents. I had never been in Holon before, and I lost my way a couple of times before I found the café Sergeant Yossi Talmon had designated as our meeting place.

Talmon had a square face framing wide cheekbones, a bulbous nose, and a wide chin. His brown eyes were melancholy and tired and topped by ruler-straight eyebrows and a tall forehead. His brown beard and mustache could have used a trim, while his hair was cropped so short I could see the pink of his scalp through it. A black tie hung loosely around his neck. He had rolled the sleeves of his white button-down shirt to his meaty biceps. I glanced at his forearm and saw no number on it.

He looked me over when I arrived, scratching at the hair on his cheek.

"I gotta tell you, Mr. Lapid, if it weren't for Reuben Tzanani asking me personally, I wouldn't be talking to you."

"I know," I said, sitting down. "I appreciate it." To show how much I did, I placed one palm down on the table. Peeking from beneath my fingers was a five-lira note.

He glanced at the note and smiled wearily. "That won't be necessary. I am not talking to you for money. You were a policeman, Reuben told me."

"In Hungary. Before the war in Europe."

"You certainly know how things are done. Not that I am a saint or anything. Normally, I would take whatever money you put in my hand—with what they pay us, it is to be expected. I have my limits, of course. No amount of money will make me cover up a rape or an arson or a murder." He sighed, rubbing his forehead. "But this time I'd prefer to keep things…pure. As much as they can be. You can put the five liras to use by paying for the beers."

I ordered a beer for myself and another for him. I handed the note to the bored-looking, lanky waiter. The café was a small place on the ground floor of a three-story water-marked building in the center of Holon. Not that the center was much to speak of.

A few shuttered stores. A post office. A health clinic. Five or six benches ringing a small copse of trees, one of which sported a vacant tire swing over a sand pit.

The interior of the café was cramped, badly lit, and smelled of cigarettes and cheap beer. The windows were smudged near the edges. Our table wobbled on uneven legs. It was the sort of place that didn't try too hard to attract customers. It had few competitors in its vicinity. It could depend on the locals to keep it going in its unambitious mediocrity. There were six tables in total. Besides our own, only one other table was occupied. We would probably need to talk fast or be asked to leave when they closed for the night. The days ended early in Holon. Here people worked hard, went to bed early, and got up early the next day to go to work again.

I looked at Talmon. His eyes were downcast, staring at the ring of condensation his beer glass had left on the table. He was smudging it with his forefinger. Or maybe he was looking at something else entirely. Something that wasn't really there. When he told me to meet him in Holon, I was sure he was after a payoff. Not that he should have gone to the trouble. I knew for a fact that policemen in Tel Aviv, like policemen in Budapest, like policemen all over the world, I imagined, received money wherever it was given them, including at their desk in the police station.

But there was another reason, apparently, and it was something that was souring his mood. Talmon looked worn, not just tired. It was more than the fatigue hard work could induce. It was something that was weighing on him from within, burdening his soul or conscience.

We sat in silence until the waiter brought our drinks and my change. He had not asked me what kind of beer I wanted, so they probably served only one kind. It was light in tone, bitter in taste, and mixed with a good deal of water. I put it down on the table at some distance from me, meaning not to touch it again.

Talmon saw my motion and smiled. "It's not much, is it? Not like what they serve in Tel Aviv. Two cities, less than five kilometers between them, and it's like a different country. Well, at least it's cold. By the way, the food here is better, if you're hungry."

I shook my head, placing the change the waiter had given me on the table. "But you can have some if you want."

"No. Not hungry either. You want to talk about Maryam Jamalka?"

"Yes."

"Reuben told me you work as a detective. You're working on this? Who's your client?"

"I'd rather not say."

"It has to be the brother. Ahmed. The one with the ugly scar on his cheek. Persistent bastard. Kept calling me and asking how the case was going, what leads did I have, did I have a suspect in mind, how long before I arrested someone? He even came by the station, came right up to my desk and demanded to see the investigation material. I thought he would take a swing at me when I told him he couldn't see it. It has to be him. I'm right, aren't I?"

His eyes were keen and perceptive. I got the sense that he was pretty good at his job. Hiding this kind of thing from him would be pointless. "You're right."

"Sure I'm right. No one else gives a damn about Maryam Jamalka. Her brother is a nag and asks too many questions for his own good, but at least he cares about her."

"What do you mean, he asks too many questions?"

But it was like Talmon did not hear me. He kept talking along a different track. "He's the only one of her family who ever called me, you know that? He was the one who came to identify her in the morgue and collect the body for burial. Not her father, not her older brothers. He took care of everything. I got to admire that. The damn bothersome fool."

"Why did you say that he asks too many questions for his own good?"

"Because you don't need to be Sherlock Holmes to know who killed his sister. He's living with them in his home up north."

"The brothers."

"Sure, the brothers. Who else?"

"Ahmed Jamalka is certain they didn't do it."

Talmon snorted. "What makes him think so? They got an alibi? Don't tell me, they were delivering soup for poor people, or were they volunteering at the local hospital?"

"No alibi that I know of. He says they told him they didn't do it."

"And he believes them?"

I nodded. "Yes. He does."

"Well," Talmon said, pointing a finger at me, "in that case, he's even a bigger fool than I thought. Let me tell you something about those two brothers of his, Jalal and Kadir. The older is thirty-five, the younger thirty-three, and both were arrested for the first time twenty years ago, in 1929, when they were still teenagers. They robbed a store in Nazareth. I saw the arrest report. They beat up the proprietor. Broke his cheekbone. And that's not the only time they got in trouble with the law. Jalal spent a year in prison for assault. Kadir got six months for another robbery. And they would have done more time if their father wasn't an important man."

"Important how?"

"He's the leader of their clan, their village—their hamoulah, as they call it. It's something between an extended family and a tribe. Don't ask me precisely what it means or how it works. But his position is such that they got off easy some of the times and got off with nothing the other times."

He paused, took another sip, and wiped his mouth with a hard pull of the back of his hand, like he had just eaten something rotten. His lower lip was thrust out when he thought about the two Jamalka brothers. His brown eyes narrowed to menacing slits. He was agitated, angry. It was the natural distaste policemen everywhere had for criminals, especially those with the money, position, or power to get away with their crimes with a slap on the wrist, or not even that.

"And their sister isn't the first person they killed. Both the British and we have them down for the murders of some of their associates or competitors in various criminal enterprises. No evidence, nothing for a court to act on. But you know how it is, sometimes a policeman just knows."

I knew what he meant. Back in Hungary there were cases, often the most frustrating ones of all, when I had to watch a criminal go free despite being certain of his guilt. It rankled. It kept me up at night sometimes. I told myself that it was the price one paid for living in a civilized society, a society based on the rule of law. But sometimes it just wasn't very convincing. And I hadn't believed it at all since the war.

"If you have any evidence—"

"Pfff. Evidence. Of course I haven't got any evidence. I've got nothing, and I'm not about to get anything, either. The case is not going anywhere. There is no investigation."

I looked at him. "What do you mean?"

"I mean," he said, tugging his beard with quick, hard pulls, "that I have done nothing to solve this murder. Well, that's not entirely true. I did work on it for the first two days after she was found and identified. There was an autopsy, not that one was needed to determine cause of death, and I did some background work on her, but that's it." He leaned forward and lowered his voice. "I was ordered to lay off it. No more work was to be done on this case."

"Who ordered you?"

"The word came down from upstairs. I got it from my inspector. And he probably got it from the chief inspector, and so on up the chain of command. I don't know how high it went. I asked, but Rosen—that's the name of my inspector, Avi Rosen—told me it was none of my business, but that it came from way up high, so I better make no trouble. Play along is what he told me. Don't make waves. Just forget about it and move on to another case. Easy for him to say, he didn't see her body. He didn't even read the report, I bet."

Talmon's voice had taken on a rough edge. Like a guard dog whose leash was too short to engage a robber, he was prevented from doing his job, and he couldn't even bark his lungs out in frustration. Now I knew why he'd gotten so upset when Reuben asked him about this case.

"Did Rosen give you a reason for the order?"

Talmon's upper lip curled, pulling his mustache down with it. "He said one thing to the medical examiner and the responding officers at the scene and another thing to me. Them, he told to be quiet so as not to cause a panic while the investigation was in progress. And I think that's what he told the woman who discovered the body. He couldn't feed me this lie. He had to tell me the truth."

He paused and took a big swallow of beer before saying, "It's the father again, Rashid Jamalka. Or rather his position. And his actions during the war. You see, when the war between us and the Arabs started in 1947, before the British left, the Jamalka clan took part in attacks on Jewish towns and vehicles. This continued well into 1948, when Syria, Egypt, Transjordan, and the rest of the Arab armies joined the war. But when it became apparent that things were not turning out as well as the Arabs had planned, that the foreign Arab armies were not about to wipe us out, he switched sides. He became an ally." Talmon made quotation marks in the air, to signify what he thought of this "ally."

He took a long gulp from the beer and wiped his beard.

"So now I'm told that I should let this investigation die a slow death of neglect, because someone higher up doesn't want to ruffle Rashid Jamalka's feathers. Because the war may be over, but who knows if it won't start up again. We want to come to some accommodation with the local Arabs, and we need clan leaders like Rashid Jamalka on our side. So what if two of his sons are common criminals? As long as they keep it relatively small, we can take it. So what if they murdered their sister? It's a family matter. It's their culture. For the sake of peace and coexistence, I should let this go."

He drained the rest of the beer, setting the glass down so hard I thought it might shatter in his hand. His face was twisted into a mask of disgust. When he spoke, it was like he was spitting the words out.

"Coexistence. With murderers? What for? Let the Arab murderers coexist in prison with the Jewish murderers where they belong. Maybe then the rest of us will find it easier to get along."

I let him get it all out. He was red across the cheeks. Suddenly he looked tired again, his pent-up energy having been discharged like the air out of a torn balloon.

"So you see," he said, in a soft, defeated voice, "this is why the investigation is dead."

I said nothing, just looked at him. He gave me a half smile that was as devoid of humor as the desert is of fish.

"I see it there, the contempt in your eyes. Don't think I don't feel a bit of it myself. You think I should have carried on, ignored the orders I'd been given. Don't think I didn't want to do just that. But Rosen's keeping an eye on me. He knows I'm not happy with the way things are. And he's a mean son of a bitch. Wouldn't hesitate to bump me off the case if he caught wind of me investigating further. He might do worse. I might end up directing traffic on Allenby Street before I got anything tangible. Or maybe I'd get kicked off the force entirely. And I have a family to feed." He let out a heavy sigh. "No, I can't do anything." He paused, looking at me. "But maybe you can."

# 9

Now I understood why Talmon had me come to Holon to meet him at this dismal café. He didn't want to be seen with me. He wanted no one to know he was talking to anyone about the case, least of all a detective who had been hired to investigate it.

Talmon said, "Reuben told me you weren't just a policeman in Hungary, but also a detective."

"That's right," I said. I had been the first and only Jewish police detective in Hungary. Not that it helped me any. First I was kicked off the force when anti-Jewish laws came into effect in the late 1930s, then I was conscripted to a hard-labor regiment and sent to dig ditches and pave roads, and finally, in 1944, I was pushed into a crowded train car, along with my family, and transported to Auschwitz. I was the only member of my family to survive the camp. I didn't tell Talmon all this. It was irrelevant, and he wouldn't have understood any of it, anyway.

"Well, this case deserves a detective," he said. "One not hampered by the chain of command and the realities of local politics. I can't do it, no matter how much I want to. But you don't have anyone above you who can order you to back off. In fact, no one even knows you've been hired to investigate this case, and no one, apart from Reuben Tzanani, knows you and I are meeting. We should keep it that way. Agreed?"

I said that it was.

He reached down and brought up a small jute bag that had been leaning against the leg of the table. He slid it toward me. Inside was something rectangular, an inch or so thick.

"Here is the complete report on the murder of Maryam Jamalka. It's not a whole lot, but it's a starting point, and who knows where you can go with it. If I were you, I would start with her record."

"She had a record?" I asked.

"Yes. That's how we identified the body. By her fingerprints."

"What was the charge?"

He averted his eyes. "It's all in the report. I can't add anything to it, since I'd done absolutely no work in that direction before Rosen told me to back off. Besides, it's getting late and we need to get out of here before they throw us out. But when you read the record, you'll see why I am dead certain those two brothers, Jalal and Kadir, are the ones who killed her."

He paused, drawing in a breath.

"One more thing. It's about the pictures in the report. They're not easy to see. They did a number on her, the savages. Consider yourself lucky that you didn't have to examine her body. The pictures capture most of it, but not everything, especially not the smell."

I didn't tell him that the sight of death did not bother me. I had seen dead bodies by the thousands. I had seen men whose bodies had been starved to a mere skeleton. I had seen men ravaged by typhoid and other diseases. I had seen men fall prey to terminal exhaustion and despair. I had seen men hanged or shot or beaten to death. I had seen men who seemed healthy enough drop dead in mid-step. I had smelled the stench of burning flesh that blew across the camp from the crematoriums. And at the end of the war, when wide-eyed American boys rescued us and served us food, I had seen men eat themselves to death, their deprived stomachs unable to handle the sudden influx of food.

A picture of a dead girl would not disturb me. But the fact of her death did.

Talmon said, "Don't open it now. Take it home with you. Read it through tonight. I want it back by tomorrow." He gave me his address and told me to stick the entire thing in his mailbox. "Tell no one you have it or that you read it."

I laid my hand on the bag. "If, after reading this, I have any questions…"

"Then you'll have to answer them yourself," he said flatly. "Don't come to me. The moment our meeting is concluded, I am out of this."

"And if I find proof as to who did it? What do you want me to do?"

Talmon smiled bitterly. "I want you to blow this whole thing wide open. Find proof, give it to a reporter, make it public. Don't give it to anyone from the department. They'll sweep it under some bureaucratic carpet. But if conclusive evidence is presented to the public, if it's out there where everyone can see it, they won't be able to keep this quiet. We will have to do our job and arrest them." He looked at me, and there was pleading in his eyes. "And I hope to God you succeed, because this girl deserves better."

I looked at him and nodded my commitment.

Outside, he led me to a white Fiat parked at the curb. "I'm sorry, but I can only take you as far as Jaffa."

"That's all right," I said, and it was. Walking was no hardship. Not on a mild night like this, without a trace of rain or sleet or snow, not with good shoes and a stomach that had seen proper food that day.

We rode in nervous silence. We hardly knew each other and we were engaged in a conspiracy of sorts. Maybe Talmon was wondering whether he had done the right thing in giving me the report. Maybe it was on the tip of his tongue to ask for it back and tell me to forget all about it. If it was, the words never came out. Which was good, because I didn't think I would have given it back.

After ten minutes or so he dropped me off on Yerushalayim Boulevard close to the Basa soccer stadium. He apologized again for not taking me further north, and I told him not to worry about it.

"Good luck," he said, and looked relieved, as if he had passed on a heavy load to me. I nodded and he drove off. I tucked the bag with the report under my arm and started walking north.

Yerushalayim Boulevard was a main thoroughfare that cut through Jaffa from north to south. Sandwiched between the south and northbound traffic lanes was a walkway lined with ficus trees. I trekked up the walkway, treading buckling paving stones, dislodged from their mooring by fist-wide roots. I continued north on the seaside road, past the forlorn turret of the Hassan Bek Mosque, all the way to Opera Square, where I took a right to Allenby. I followed it as it curled southeast and cut my way through a number of side streets till I got to Hamaccabi Street and my apartment.

I drank two glasses of water, took a long shower, and got into some clean clothes. With a hot cup of tea to keep me company, I sat at my dining table, took out the folder Yossi Talmon had given me, and weighed it in my hands. I burst out laughing. The previous day I had asked myself why I should stick my neck out for Ahmed Jamalka, and here I was, doing just that. I was pursuing a case the police higher-ups wanted dead and buried and forgotten, and I was in possession of a police report I had no business reading. I was probably breaking some laws, and I knew the police could come down hard on me. So why was I doing it? Why get involved? Why take the risk?

I wasn't doing it for Ahmed Jamalka, I realized. I was doing it for his sister. Because she was dead. Because she deserved better. Because someone had to do it. And because no one else would.

I flipped open the folder and began reading the murder report of the almost-forsaken Maryam Jamalka.

# 10

Maryam Jamalka's body was discovered by a Mrs. Olga Gal, a sixty-six-year-old resident of Tel Aviv, who was taking her regular early morning walk along the southern bank of the Yarkon River. She began her trek at the corner of Ibn Gabirol and Ussishkin Streets and walked west toward the sea. She would usually walk all the way to the mouth of the river, spend a few minutes admiring the tower of the Reading Power Station, which stood on the opposite bank, then retrace her steps before going to eat breakfast in her apartment on Alexander Yannai Street.

It was a comforting and healthy routine, one which Mrs. Gal had adhered to for a good many years. Rain or shine, she told the officer, she always took her walk. But on the nineteenth of September, 1949, she cut her trek short when, where an outcropping of earth hid part of the Yarkon's bank from view, she came upon the naked body of a young black-haired woman.

The body was lying with its lower half submerged in the brackish water of the river and its face sunk into the soft, wet earth of the bank. Here Mrs. Gal—whose body had been made strong by her early years as a farm girl and her later years as the

59

mother of four strapping boys—did something that Sergeant Talmon ardently wished that she hadn't: She grabbed Maryam Jamalka's body by the armpits and dragged it out of the water and up the slope of the bank.

Mrs. Gal could see that the young woman was dead. The gash across her neck was sufficiently wide to be visible even in a prone position. So Mrs. Gal did not try to revive her nor did she turn her over. She did, however, perform one additional act of charity—she removed her shirt and used it to cover the corpse's exposed buttocks, tucking the sleeves under the thighs to make sure the shirt wouldn't be carried off by a stray breeze. Unfortunately, that left Mrs. Gal in nothing but her skirt and girdle and shoes, and she was not the sort to walk around immodestly dressed. Nevertheless, she did not rush straight home for another shirt. Instead, she hurried back to Ibn Gabirol Street, ignoring the stares of the few people on the street at that early hour, located a telephone, and called the police. Only then did she go home, put on a shirt and grab a small star-embroidered blanket her grandchildren used when they came over to visit. She went back to where she'd found the dead woman and covered her naked back with the blanket. Then she stood watch over the body, ready to fight off any voyeur who might have passed by. In the end, no such person came. Some minutes later, two policemen found a clench-fisted Mrs. Gal shaking with fury that such an indignity might befall a woman in her beloved Tel Aviv.

Mrs. Gal's humanity went against investigative protocol, which called for the preservation of a crime scene until it had been scoured for evidence. Upon arriving at the scene, Talmon conducted an extensive interview with Mrs. Gal, lobbing question after question at her, all for the purpose of determining whether she had inadvertently erased any evidence the killer might have left behind—footprints, cigarette butts, a wrapper of food, a torn button. Judging by her answers, Mrs. Gal quickly wearied of this line of questioning and made it clear to Sergeant Talmon that, regardless of what he thought of her, she was not a careless fool and would not have disturbed any evidence. As for his insinuation that she had disrupted the crime scene by pulling the body from the water, she was not only unapologetic, but also proud of her actions. It was the right thing to do. The girl was dead and what she had seen of her body left no doubt that she had been violently murdered. Leaving her in the water for the fish or river rats to feast on was out of the question, evidence be damned. I smiled when I pictured the sad-eyed Talmon on the receiving end of the righteous fury of Mrs. Gal. And despite the dry and factual tone of his report, I was certain that Talmon did not resent her reproach.

Mrs. Gal was questioned as to the position of the body when she had found it, and a sketch was made and included in the report. I studied it but could see little to be gleaned from it.

Ample pictures of the spot in which Mrs. Gal had first seen the body were taken. They showed little apart from the drag marks Maryam Jamalka's corpse had made as it was being pulled to dry land. Nothing could be learned from them. At that point, Mrs. Gal was returned her blanket and shirt and thanked for doing her civic duty by calling the police.

An additional set of pictures was taken of the body as it now lay. They were what one would expect—cold and morbid and lifeless and empty. Maryam Jamalka's hair was plastered to the sides of her face and neck like seaweed to the pilings of a pier. Her dark skin had been bleached to a filmy paleness by her blood loss and her time in the water. Her complexion was like marble that had been smudged with soot. Only the edge of her neck wound could be seen, but it was dark and deep and obviously fatal.

The police placed an open body bag beside the corpse. Talmon then did a sensible thing. He ordered the two patrolmen who had first come to the scene to position themselves at some distance from the body and establish a perimeter that no civilian could breach. He and the photographer and the medical examiner were the only ones to see the front of the body after they had turned it over onto the body bag.

Another set of pictures was taken of the body in its new position. It showed far more than the previous set had. I looked at each picture carefully, soaking in all the details I could absorb. Apart from the wounds themselves, there was very little blood on the body, most of it having been washed away by the river. Her eyes were half open, a moon-sliver of white bordered at the top with the brown of her irises. Her full lips drooped and there was a slackness to her skin that not even sleep could bring. Where she hadn't been cut, that was.

Her cheeks and forehead were marked by a large number of cuts, none longer than an inch, and none that looked deep. These cuts were not what had ended her life. They'd been put there for another reason. To inflict pain or induce horror or simply to disfigure her face. I looked at the head shot of Maryam Jamalka that her brother had given me. My mind could tell it was the same person, but something on the inside, about where my stomach was, rebelled against the identification. I remembered people in Auschwitz, both the living and the dead, who had aroused the same feeling in me. There were times they did not seem like real men to me. Real men could not look as they did— as I did, too. They were too thin, haggard, dirty, lost. You would not see their kind on the streets of Budapest or Tel Aviv or Munich, or any other city, town, or village. In Auschwitz, the feeling was spread among the thousands I saw. Here it was focused on a single dead woman. The smiling Maryam Jamalka was the naked corpse in the black body bag. There was no doubt of that. But it was wrong. It was something that should not have been true.

I closed my eyes for a moment, thinking of the dead females in my life. My mother, my sisters, my wife, my daughters. The memory brought with it the familiar, raw pain. I clenched my teeth, shook my head, and shoved the memory down into the recesses of my mind. I opened my eyes and looked at more pictures of the dead Maryam Jamalka.

The major wounds were in her torso and neck. Five wounds in total: four stab wounds—two in the stomach, two in the chest —and a gaping slash across the neck. All had left dark-red gashes in her skin. Ugly puckering wounds, like earth-torn bomb craters in a grassy field. Her legs and chest and belly had not been spared. They bore a large number of shallow cuts, similar to the ones on her face, all the way from her collarbones to her ankles.

I could well understand why the medical examiner had refused to show Ahmed Jamalka more of his sister's body than was absolutely necessary for an identification. This was not a sight most people could handle well. Especially when a family member was in question. Mrs. Gal was made of sturdy stuff indeed, but had the body been supine instead of prone, she might not have been able to act as coolly as she did.

I sat back, took a long sip of tea, rubbed some stiffness out of my neck, and took a few deep breaths before returning my gaze to the pictures.

This was a passionate killing rather than a crime of passion. In the latter, the killer was driven to a reckless act, moved by an overwhelming rush of emotion; in the first, the passion did not erupt in a single unplanned burst. It was a controlled, premeditated, thought-out murder. In the latter there was shock, remorse, regret, a desire for it all to be a nightmare; in the first, there was a joy in killing, a fulfillment of a dream rather than the suffering of a nightmare.

A few questions arose: Was Maryam Jamalka killed where she had been found? If not, did the killer dump her body there or at some other point along the Yarkon? Had he hoped that her body would be washed out to sea? Was it a single killer or a number of them? Was Talmon correct in placing the blame on the two brothers, their denials to Ahmed Jamalka notwithstanding?

Once enough pictures had been taken, the police closed the body bag and loaded it into a car. It was taken to the morgue, where an autopsy was performed. The autopsy determined a number of facts: there was no water in Maryam Jamalka's lungs, meaning that she did not drown, meaning that she was dead before being placed in the water. Three of the five deep cuts could have been fatal by themselves. One had punctured the heart, another sliced the liver nearly in two, and the neck wound would have bled her out in less than a minute. The order of the wounds could not be determined. By the angles of the wounds, the medical examiner concluded that the killer was right-handed and that he'd used both upper and lower thrusts. This, I thought, meant that the killer had paused to adjust his grip on the knife, lending support to my intuition that this was not some on-the-spur-of-the-moment murder, but a calculated attack.

The medical examiner counted the number of cuts on the body. Apart from the five major wounds, there were fifty-one slashes and cuts, some very shallow, probably done as an afterthought and with a quick flick of the wrist, and others longer and slightly deeper, likely done slowly and with intention. There was no pattern to the cuts. They did not describe a shape or combine into a word or symbol.

He methodically examined each cut. Some had bled, most had not. This meant that some of the cuts had been done pre-mortem and others postmortem. The killer had taken his time with her. He wanted to leave his mark on her, and was willing to take the risk of being around a dead body for longer than neces-sary to do so. Even though it meant nothing to us, it did mean something to him. It was possible that there was nothing specific to be read in the arrangement of the cuts. Perhaps he simply enjoyed damaging her.

More pictures were taken of the body. In the glaring light of the morgue, the skin shone with a harsh brilliance. Maryam had a small birthmark on her left shoulder. Its shape resembled a bird in flight.

The medical examiner noted what I had already learned from the earlier pictures—the back and buttocks of the corpse were undamaged. Why this was so remained an open question in a sea of them.

He continued with a more in-depth examination. He examined her fingernails and found them to be in good condition, with no traces of skin underneath them. He noted that such traces could have been washed away by the river, but he doubted it, considering the slow flow of the Yarkon. Her wrists and ankles showed no rope marks or signs of other restraint. She had food content in her stomach. Bread and cheese and vegetables. The medical examiner estimated that she had been in the water for less than twelve hours and dead no more than twice that.

I finished reading the medical examination report. I drank the rest of my tea and got up to put the cup in the kitchen sink. I came back to the living room, lit a cigarette, and stood by the window, letting the smoke filter out to the street and curl up into the inky, starred sky.

My mind drifted back to my meeting with Yossi Talmon. I could appreciate his rage. As a policeman you quickly learned that, while the law might group them all under a single category, murders came in a variety of shapes and forms and degrees of severity. Some were relatively clean—a gunshot to the head, a push off a tall building, a knife in the heart—you got used to those. They became part of the job, and only the job. Other murders were acts of such evil and savagery that they screamed for justice in a voice that could invade your dreams. What had been done to Maryam Jamalka was such an act. I thought of Talmon. He had seemed tired when we met. Was his sleep infested with nightmares? Was he kept awake by guilt, knowing that he was doing nothing to solve this murder?

I gritted my teeth. This murder deserved a whole team of detectives, the full resources of the police, until it was solved. But it didn't have a single policeman working on it. All it had was me. And if I couldn't find this killer, then no one ever would.

I snuffed out my cigarette, lit another, and stood in the window some more, watching the silent street below, the dark buildings across the road. People were asleep in those buildings, unaware that such a brutal murder had taken place in their city.

A thought came to me: Should I go to the press with what I learned? I decided that it would be risky and pointless. Any story about the murder would either have to list me as a source or keep the source anonymous. In the latter case, Inspector Rosen and those higher-ups who gave the order not to pursue the case would naturally suspect Yossi Talmon of being the source. Even if I were willing to be named as the source of the story, Rosen would go after Talmon, suspecting that he had fed me the information. Either way, it would likely cost Talmon his career. It would be a betrayal of the faith he had placed in me by showing me the file.

And this sacrifice would be for nothing, for little would change. The police would flatly deny shelving the investigation. They would say that they were hard at work at it. And soon a new story would claim the headlines and the police could go back to doing absolutely nothing.

No, going to the press at this time was not the answer. As Talmon had said, I needed to present proof of the killer's identity to force the police to act. And Talmon's certainty notwithstanding, there was no proof linking the Jamalka brothers to the murder of their sister. Unlike Ahmed Jamalka, I was not convinced of their innocence, but by taking his case, I had committed to maintaining an open mind on the matter, and so I would.

I smoked the cigarette all the way through, stubbed it out on the windowsill, and went back to my table. I proceeded to summarize the important findings so far in my notebook. Tomorrow I would return the report to Talmon and would likely never be given access to it again. I needed to get all the pertinent information in my notebook, and in my mind, before morning came.

I was tired, and I found myself casting longing glances toward my bed. But I had to get this done. I would have to catch up on my sleep tomorrow.

There was a good chance I would miss things. An investigation was like that. You absorbed a great number of details and you could never be sure which of them would end up being crucial. Some minor thing, some seemingly inconsequential fact, could turn out to be the key to a solution, and I might fail to note it in my summary. I took copious notes, looked over all the pictures again, read the medical report once more, and hoped I was getting everything I would need.

Once I had a detailed summary of what I'd read so far, I went back to the report. And I learned why Talmon had told me to start with Maryam Jamalka's record. It was short enough to read in less than a minute, and I wondered if Ahmed Jamalka knew about his sister's history. I doubted it. It further supported Talmon's theory that Jalal and Kadir Jamalka were behind the murder. It appeared that Maryam's transgressions against the honor of her family went beyond an illicit love affair. She had been arrested. The arrest had taken place a mere three weeks before her death, and she had spent the three days following it in a jail cell.

The charge was solicitation. Maryam Jamalka had been a

prostitute. I could think of little that would bring more shame upon her family.

———

I copied the details of the arrest—date, name of arresting officer, the outcome of the arrest, the case number—into my notebook. Talmon had advised me to start with her record. But there were many possible roads stretching from this starting point. And a wide range of possible killers. A prostitute faced a greater danger of being killed than most people did. Their work involved being alone with strange men, most of whom were physically stronger than they were. It was not easy to determine at a glance which men were just interested in sex and which harbored darker fantasies. It was a skill prostitutes developed with time and bad experience. The killer could be a client, and he could also be a disgruntled pimp whom the prostitute had tried to flee. Another option was that the killer was not a man Maryam Jamalka had known professionally, but someone who specifically sought out a prostitute to kill, knowing that it would be easy to get her alone. A man who simply wanted to kill a woman.

I piled the papers and pictures back into the file and put it in the jute bag. A glance at my watch revealed that it was past three o'clock. I was tired and my muscles ached. I rose and stretched my arms and shoulders. I went to the window again but did not light another cigarette. Outside, the street was dark and still. No animal or human sound came to my ears. The cool night air seemed to be sleeping. It stood motionless, like an inhalation right before its discharge.

The quiet disturbed me. It did not seem right that with an unsolved brutal murder in our city, my neighbors, and even the elements, were unperturbed. Of course, they hadn't seen the pictures I had. They did not even know that Maryam Jamalka had ever been alive, let alone that she was dead. That was how most deaths went—especially the brutal ones of lonely and helpless people. They caused not a ripple, made not a sound, left not a trace in the minds of most people.

I ran a hand over my eyes. They were heavy and my whole body felt the need for sleep. I shut the window, turned off the light, and, in the darkness that fell, removed my clothes and got into bed. I waited for the nightmares to come. They did not keep me waiting for long.

# 11

I got out of bed shortly before ten, shaved, had a quick breakfast, and left the apartment with the jute bag under my arm. I walked to Ben Yehuda Street, found Talmon's building, and stuck the crime report in his mailbox.

The rest of the day I passed at Greta's, playing chess, drinking coffee, and listening to the other regulars discuss the dismal state of Israeli politics. I returned to my apartment shortly after eight thirty to shower and grab my jacket.

At nine o'clock I walked to the corner and got on the same bus I had taken the night I broke Charlie Buzaglo's ribs. The bus smelled of stale cigarette smoke despite all the windows being open. The driver looked tired and drove with the speed of a man who was desperate to end his shift and go home. I had my knife with me. Its weight felt comforting in my jacket pocket.

The arrest of Maryam Jamalka, a mere three weeks before she died, took place in a bar called Club Adom on Elifelet Street in the south of Tel Aviv. I was going to see if I could pick up her trail and learn more about how she had lived her life.

I got off the bus on Shalma Road and turned south onto

Elifelet Street. Near the southern tip of the street, between a drapery and a photography studio, was Club Adom. The place was large with a long bar on the right side and tables on the left. At the far end, a dozen couples danced with varying degrees of awkwardness to the sound of lively, Eastern European music that was coming from a dark-brown gramophone with a gigantic speaker. I took a seat at the bar and looked around at the patrons. There were a bit more men than women, and some of the women seemed younger than their dance partners. The scent of perfume and cologne permeated the air.

The bartender was a slim man with thinning brown hair that had been carefully parted on the left side. His face was long and lean, with a soft jaw and chin. A pencil-thin mustache topped his upper lip, and light blue eyes flanked a narrow, hooked nose. He wore a pressed white shirt and a black bow tie. He reminded me of café waiters in Budapest before the war.

"What will you have?" he asked me, bringing out a cloth and making a show of wiping clean the section of bar I had claimed as my own.

"Do you water your beer?" I asked, recalling the watery brew I had in Holon in my meeting with Yossi Talmon.

He chuckled. "These days, nothing is pure. Everything is mixed with something else. But we don't add as much as other places do."

"All right. I'll have one."

He nodded and drew me a glass. He poured it slow and well, and the foam only took up an inch near the top of the glass. I took a slow sip. "Like you said, it's not pure. But it's not totally corrupt, either."

He laughed, and I sensed that it wasn't a laugh he offered merely as part of his service. I laid some money on the bar, and when he brought back my change, I took some of it and waved at the rest.

"For you," I said, taking another long sip.

He gave a nod of thanks before sweeping the coins into his hand. They disappeared somewhere below the bar.

"You haven't been here before," he said.

"First time. This is a nice place."

The left side of his mouth curled into a smile. "I do my best."

"What else do you serve that's good?" I asked.

"You mean food or drinks?"

"Neither."

He looked at me thoughtfully. "Are you a policeman?"

"No."

"You look like a policeman."

"I've been told that."

"It's something in your eyes. Okay, so you're not a policeman. But your question didn't just come out of thin air. You know what there is to be had here."

I glanced toward the dance floor. "Are they all working girls?"

He followed my eyes. "Not all of them. Not even half of them. As you said, this is a nice place. Couples come here to drink and dance and enjoy themselves. The rest is extra. Are you looking for anything specific? I am not a pimp, you need to understand. I simply allow working girls the use of my bar."

"For a fee, I suppose."

His cheeks reddened with indignation. "As I said, I am not a pimp. I do not charge the girls anything, nor do I try to claim ownership of them. I simply offer them a safe place to operate. It is safer here than being on the streets and better than other bars as well."

"I was too quick to judge," I said. "I apologize." And I meant it. He was right, probably more than he would have guessed. The most dangerous place for a prostitute was on the street. Here, in the bar, it was well lit and there were people around. True, once she left with a client, the prostitute would once more be alone and vulnerable, but a killer might be deterred by the fact that other people had seen his face when he picked her up in the bar.

The anger left his face. "Apology accepted. The truth is that they're good for business. They draw the men in, and as long as they are not too obvious about their business, female patrons don't seem to mind too much either. But you haven't told me what sort of woman you're looking for."

I took out the photograph of Maryam Jamalka that her brother had given me and set it on the bar. I pointed at it. "This one."

He looked at the picture, then up at me, suspicious.

"You are a policeman," he said.

I shook my head. "No."

"Then why are you looking for Miryam?"

"Miryam?" I said, frowning for a moment before realizing that Miryam was the Hebrew version of the Arab name, Maryam.

He blinked, realizing he had just admitted to knowing her.

"I don't want to get her into trouble."

"She won't get into any trouble," I said, figuring it was better to keep the fact of Maryam's death to myself for now. I felt uncomfortable lying to this man but knew it might be the best way to catch her killer off guard. "Her family is looking for her."

"Maybe she doesn't want to be found. Some of these girls, they didn't have a good family life."

"She talked about her family life?"

"No. She didn't talk a lot, that one. Not with me, at least."

"But she did talk with some of the other girls," I ventured.

He looked away toward the dance floor. I considered offering him money for the information, but I decided against it. He seemed genuinely protective of the women who plied their trade in his bar. I didn't think he would open up at the sight of a coin or a banknote. In fact, he might take it as an insult. He chewed his lower lip, and a line appeared between his eyebrows.

"You're worried about her," I said. "You haven't seen her for a while."

He scrutinized my face. He seemed to like what he saw because he let out a breath, walked down the length of the bar toward the dance floor, and signaled for someone to come. A curvy, red-haired young woman disengaged herself from her dance partner with a smile and a pat on the chest and sauntered over. Her black dress clung closely to her hips and breasts and displayed a wedge of pale flesh across the top of her chest. She leaned one elbow on the bar to the left of me, and I noticed the powder that covered her cheeks, forehead, and nose. She had painted her lips with bright red lipstick. She was trying too hard to make herself more beautiful.

"What is it, Akiva?" she asked, a little exasperated. Perhaps she was about to close the deal with the man she had been dancing with. Or perhaps she had simply enjoyed his company. She looked at me, and her gaze turned businesslike. She held out a hand the way a lady would, with the back of her hand up and her fingers curled down. "Hello, I'm Lydia."

"Adam," I said. I could smell alcohol on her breath.

"Well, Adam," she said, taking a big breath that made her chest heave, "what can I do for you?"

She wasn't unattractive, but as with her makeup, she was trying too hard to be seductive. On me it had the opposite effect than the one intended. Her accent was Eastern European. Something to the east of Hungary. Ukraine, or perhaps Russia.

Akiva said, "Lydia, this man is looking for Miryam. I haven't seen her here for a few weeks. Do you know where she is?"

She turned off the charm now that she discovered I was not interested in her. She looked at the bartender. "I was sort of busy, Akiva. Surely this can wait."

I put some money on the bar. "A few minutes of conversation, right here, and this is yours."

She glanced at the money, then at Akiva. "Is he all right?"

By which she meant, could I be trusted? Akiva gave me another quick look and nodded. "I think so," he said.

Lydia shrugged. She parked herself on the stool next to mine and scooped the money into a black leather purse.

"Get me a drink, will you, Akiva?"

He gave her something clear in a short glass. She gulped it down in one swallow, grimacing. A customer called for Akiva from the other end of the bar, and he went to him, leaving Lydia and me alone.

"Haven't seen Miryam for over a month," she said.

"You two are friends?"

She gave it some thought. "Not really. We just look out for each other. We girls have to stick together." She looked at me. Her eyes were light green and a bit bleary. "You know what we do."

"Yes."

"So we need to be there for each other, because no one else will. Oh, they'll take us to bed or to the backseat of their car, if they have one. They'll buy us a drink here, a drink there, but they won't be there for us in case we actually need them. Understand?"

I nodded.

"So Miryam and I, we have a sort of deal: I keep my eye on her; she keeps her eye on me. Just to be extra safe. But we aren't friends. Come to think of it, I hardly know anything about her."

She picked up her empty glass, set it down, and looked for Akiva, who was still pouring drinks for other people who wanted to blur their minds.

"And you haven't seen her for a month," I said, drawing her back to the conversation.

"Just about. But she started coming much less frequently than she used to even sooner. Three weeks or so before I last saw her."

"Right after her arrest," I ventured a guess.

Lydia eyed me. "You know about that?"

"Yes."

"You're right, you know. I haven't thought about it till now, but it was about that time."

"About what time?" Akiva said, returning from taking care of his other patron.

"Good that you're back, Akiva," Lydia said, handing him her shot glass. "Pour me another."

He got the bottle and repeated his question. "About what time?"

"The time that Miryam was arrested," Lydia said. She poured the liquid down her throat and pointed at her glass. Akiva frowned at her, but filled it.

"I remember that night," Akiva said. "It shouldn't have happened. I have good relations with the police." He looked sheepish for an instant, and I realized what he meant was he paid someone at the police not to bother any of the girls. "It made me very angry to see one of them just grab poor Miryam and drag her out with him," he continued, "Very humiliating. And in handcuffs, too."

"He handcuffed her?" I said, frowning. "Was she resisting arrest?"

"Of course not." Lydia snorted. "She knew very well how to handle a grabby policeman. They want one of two things: cash or..." She made a graphic motion in the air with her hand. "You give it to them and they go away."

"Then why the handcuffs?"

She shrugged, and Akiva said, "I remember asking the policeman about it, and he told me to shut up, that he was just doing his job. I got the sense that he wasn't getting much pleasure out of the whole thing either."

Lydia said, "He probably did get some pleasure out of it soon after, the pig. That's what they are, the lot of them. Filthy pigs." She emptied her glass and slid it to Akiva.

He didn't pick it up, giving her a worried look. "Perhaps you've had enough to drink, Lydia."

"Not even close. I'm Russian, remember. I can drink the entire bottle without showing it."

She was showing it already. Her pronunciation had turned slurry, and her cheeks were ruddy under the makeup. With obvious reluctance, Akiva refilled Lydia's glass. She drained it in one swallow.

"Was there anything else that was strange about the night Miryam was arrested?" I asked.

Akiva thought it over. "No. Nothing much. He just led her out, and she went quietly with him."

"But she didn't come back the next day," Lydia muttered. "That was strange. Usually, you slip the policeman a little something or have him slip you a little something, and you're back here in an hour or the next night at the latest. Miryam didn't come back for more than a week."

"A week, you sure about that?" I asked, remembering from the police report that Maryam had been locked up for three days after that arrest.

"A week, or maybe even ten days," she said. "I remember thinking about it, wondering."

Akiva nodded. "She's right. I remember thinking the same thing."

"Did you try to find her?"

"Didn't know where to look. Like I said, we aren't friends. I don't know where she lives, and she doesn't know where I live, either. Miryam is private, doesn't talk much. I can't even tell you where she grew up."

That was because she didn't want you to know she was an Arab, I thought. That might have been problematic for a number of reasons. One, some of her potential clients might not have wanted to buy her services. Two, her family might have been searching for her, and being found might have cost her her life, which, if Talmon was right and Ahmed Jamalka was wrong, was precisely what had happened.

For a second the thought of telling Lydia and Akiva that Maryam was dead flashed across my mind. I wouldn't have minded admitting to the lie of not telling them straight away. But if I told, the news would spread fast. The police would know I was investigating the murder, and so might the killer.

"But she did come back after a week to ten days?" I asked.

"Yes," Lydia said. She paused and her eyebrows knitted together. "But she wasn't the same. I couldn't tell you how or why, but she seemed...distant, somehow. Less lively. And she didn't take any more clients."

"No one?"

She shook her head. "No one at all."

"She didn't say anything about her mood? About the time she was away?"

Lydia frowned. "I'm sure I asked her about it, where she was and all, but she shrugged off the question. It wasn't the first time she did that. As I said, she didn't talk a lot about herself."

"Any regular clients?"

"We all have repeats."

"No one strange? Aggressive?"

"No. No one like that," Lydia said. "We all get the shy ones, the lonely ones, those that can't find a woman for themselves. And sometimes we get those with special tastes. But I don't remember anyone aggressive or frightening who was interested specifically in Miryam."

"No one who seemed upset if she wasn't available?"

They both shook their heads. Lydia said, "If there was anyone who was bothering her, she didn't say anything."

I nodded, more to myself than to them. I was getting that dead-end feeling you got when the questions ran out and you looked around for some way to proceed and found yourself surrounded by walls.

Then Akiva said to Lydia, "You know who might know something…"

"Who?"

"Sima."

"Oh, her." Lydia rolled her eyes.

Akiva gave a half smile. "Jealousy doesn't become you, my dear."

"I am not jealous of Sima," Lydia said. But I could tell she was lying by the sharpness of her tone and the way she averted her eyes from Akiva's. She rose abruptly, saying that she needed to get back to her work, and flounced to the table where the man she'd been dancing with was waiting.

"Sima?" I asked.

"Sima Vaaknin."

"Lydia doesn't like her very much," I said.

"Sima is not usual."

"Another working girl?"

"Yes," Akiva said, and after a beat added, "But not the usual sort."

I looked toward the dance floor. There were only half a dozen couples still at it. The rest had gone back to their tables or left in search of some illicit privacy.

"Is she here?"

"Oh, no. Sima doesn't operate from here," Akiva said. "I haven't seen her in months."

"And what's her connection with Miryam?"

"She was the one who brought her here for the first time. Who introduced me to her."

A madam of sorts, I figured, but didn't say it out loud. There was something in Akiva's tone that made me think he would not appreciate a bad word or insinuation regarding Sima Vaaknin.

"How can I reach her?"

"I can give her a call on your behalf, but I can't guarantee she'll agree to speak with you. Sima is unpredictable."

He brought a phone with a long cord from underneath the bar and lifted the headset.

"You're calling her now?" I said, surprised. It was after ten o'clock.

"She won't be asleep," Akiva said.

He dialed the number but hung up after a moment. "No answer. I'll try again in fifteen minutes."

I asked, "How is it that Sima Vaaknin has a telephone at home?"

Akiva smiled. "Sima knows people."

I ordered another beer, and he went to hand out bills to some of the patrons who were calling it a night. I sipped my beer slowly, letting what I had learned from Lydia and Akiva settle in my mind. I hadn't learned much, but often information needed to sit for a while in my mind until it ripened into a clue I could use, a thread I could pull to unravel a mystery.

By the time I finished my beer, more patrons had left the bar. Almost half of the tables were now vacant, and the dance floor was deserted. Akiva went to the dance floor, turned off the music, and returned to the bar. He let out a theatrical sigh of relief and smiled at me. "Each night, after listening to the music for hours, I find that I am starved for silence."

He dialed again, and this time it was picked up. He got a silly-looking smile on his face and said, "Hello, Sima," and asked her how she was doing.

He told her that I was looking for Miryam Cohen and that he thought she might agree to meet with me. She apparently asked about me, because he started describing me to her. My height, the width of my shoulders, my facial features, my hair. It felt odd to be described that way, and I asked myself what good this information could do to her. When he was done, he listened for a moment, then hung up. He took a pen out of his pants pocket, scrawled something on a scrap of paper, handed it over, and said to me, "Here is her address. Sima says you should come tomorrow at five. She is busy tonight."

# 12

I rose the next day and had breakfast at Greta's Café. I read a couple of newspapers, learned that the world was a dangerous place and that Israel's economy was still in the doldrums. I half-listened to an impassioned argument between two other patrons, one of whom was a communist who believed that Stalin was the greatest man who ever lived, the other a former officer in the Polish Army who fought the Russians in 1920 and thought the mustached tyrant of Moscow was the devil incarnate. I played a quick game of chess with myself and chatted with Greta at the bar. She said I looked tired. I said I didn't feel it. No more than usual.

Before noon I left Greta's and wandered over to a small cobbler's shop on Shefer Street. The potbellied man who ran the store knew I wasn't there to get my shoes fixed. He disappeared into a back room and came back with a cone-shaped paper-wrapped package as long and wide as my forearm. The scent of sausage, paprika, black pepper, and garlic wafted through the paper. The smell made my mouth water. Meat was strictly rationed, and I had no idea where he got his supply. His wife did the seasoning herself, and they probably made more money by selling sausage on the black market than he did by fixing shoes and selling laces and polish.

He handed me the roll of sausage, and I handed him a banknote. The money went straight into his pocket. I asked for a bag and he gave me one. I put the sausage in it and walked out. I went back to my apartment and ate two pieces of bread with thick slices of sausage. The rest I put in my icebox.

After I'd eaten, I stripped to my shorts and lay in my bed. I had a Western paperback with a promising cover of two gunmen in leather chaps and wide-brimmed cowboy hats, facing each other across a dusty street. I started reading and by page five felt my eyes grow heavy like paperweights. I closed my eyes, thinking to let them rest for a few minutes, and woke up three and a half hours later, with the book resting open in the shape of an army tent on the sheet beside me.

I took a shower, ate some more bread, emptied my can of coffee beans into a glass, filled it with hot water, and drank the combination, black and bitter. Then I headed out.

Sima Vaaknin lived on the second floor of a white Bauhaus building on a quiet, tree-lined street in the north of Tel Aviv, as far as one could get from the club where Maryam Jamalka was arrested. It was not the sort of place one imagined a prostitute would live. But then Akiva had said that Sima Vaaknin was different.

At five on the dot, I knocked on the door, and it was whisked open as if she had been waiting just on the other side. The woman who stood in the opening could have been sixteen or seventeen years old.

For a moment I was unable to utter a word. I could well understand why Lydia would be jealous of Sima Vaaknin. She had a natural beauty and appeal I had only rarely encountered. Men would want to have her, and women would want to have what she had. She was five foot five, and every line of her body soared and sank where it should have. She was wearing a calf-length bright-yellow dress of some thin material through which the dark skin of her thighs and belly could be intimated. The cloth was thicker around the breasts and hips and groin, but that concealment only added to her appeal. A red sash belted the dress at her waist, accentuating its narrowness and the fullness of her breasts and hips. Below the hem of the dress, her feet were bare, her ankles thin and delicate. Above the neckline, the skin was flawless and the color of caramel. Her collarbones were shapely, her neck long and taut, her shoulders nicely rounded.

The grin she offered me dominated her face. Her teeth sparkled between thick and shapely unlipsticked lips that were a reddish pink, and in both cheeks deep dimples appeared. Her eyes were large and wide-set. Their color was a dark-brown like moist and fertile farmland. Her hair was black and brilliant and thick. It hung around her face and shoulders like a burst of ink. It was the sort of hair to run your hand through, to stroke gently, and, at certain moments, to grip hard in your hand.

I could tell by the widening of her smile that she was aware of my reaction to her appearance and was enjoying my discomfort.

I asked if she was Sima Vaaknin.

"Who else? Haven't you come here specifically to meet me?" she said, her voice high-pitched and playful.

She turned and walked deeper into the apartment, leaving the door open for me. I entered, closing the door behind me, following the sway of her hips as she made her way down the short hall to the living room. She had the lazy, flowing movement of a satisfied cat. With a gesture of her hand, she wordlessly offered me the choice of a sofa and two armchairs.

I took one of the chairs. She remained standing, now looking down at me from beneath her long curling eyelashes.

"I have wine and coffee and tea and water. What would you like?"

I told her water would be fine. She went and fetched it. The glass was cold, filled with ice. As she handed it to me, I could smell the scent of jasmine and cinnamon on her skin. I emptied the glass. The water felt fantastic. She took the used glass from me. She had brought nothing for herself.

She sat on the sofa, bending her feet under her.

"So you're Adam," she said.

"Yes. Adam Lapid."

"You're almost exactly like Akiva described you. But your eyes are a lighter green, and your hair a darker brown. He also didn't mention that troubled expression you wear."

"I look troubled?"

"There's a line between your eyebrows that looks as permanent as a scar. That's all right, though. It suits you. And I sort of like scars."

"Are you always this direct?"

She nodded. "Especially with men."

She smiled, one hand flattening the fabric of her dress along her thigh with a long, smooth motion. Then she tilted her head slightly backward and raised both hands, pushing her hair back past her ears. The movement made her dress stretch taut across her chest, and I could clearly make out the outline of her breasts. Then she lowered her hands back to her thighs, letting her hair fall back to where it had been, and the fabric of her dress loosened, better hiding what lay beneath. As far as I could see, her hair had not needed adjustment, and her dress had not required smoothing. I got the sense that nothing Sima Vaaknin did, not a single movement of her limbs or a curl of her lips or her intonation, was without purpose. It was all designed to draw and shift my eyes and attention from one body part to the next. Teasing my eyes with her legs, then her breasts, then her neck, then her face, then her mouth, and back to her legs again. And unlike Lydia's crude maneuvers, Sima Vaaknin did not appear to be trying too hard. In fact, she did not look like she was making any effort whatsoever. Her enticing movements were as natural as breathing and walking.

And it was working. I could feel a tingle across my body, not just by looking at her, but also by being looked at by her. I realized I had shifted in my seat under her stare and drew my body straighter. I took a big breath, made myself sit still, and managed to tear my eyes away from her. I let my gaze wander about the room.

It was clean and the walls looked freshly painted. A gramophone sat on a chest of drawers along one wall, and records were stacked by its side. White, lacy curtains were drawn across the doors to the balcony, lightly shifting in the breeze. A large thick rug lay under the long, rectangular coffee table that squatted between the chair where I sat and the sofa on which Sima Vaaknin reclined. There were pictures on the wall, all bright colors and happy themes. Open seas, peasants consuming a feast, birds soaring across an azure sky. My eyes latched on one picture in particular. Three white-dressed children cavorting in a sun-soaked field of bright orange and yellow flowers, a bright-blue stream coursing to the right. And in the distance, a mother watching over them all, her posture that of parental satisfaction.

"You can tell me, if you like," she said, drawing my attention back to her.

"Tell you what?"

"What's troubling you."

She was peering at me, her face unreadable. Or perhaps I detected a trace of curiosity there. But no more than that. Certainly not the concern her invitation suggested she felt.

I wondered how old she really was. Her face had the freshness of a teenager, her body the litheness of adolescence, her smile the guilelessness of youth. But she was obviously no teenager. She had insight born of years and experience.

I considered telling her that she was wrong, that nothing was troubling me, but I didn't bother with the lie. She would see right through it. I imagined that she had seen men lie a good number of times before in her life. Too many times to be fooled.

"But that's not why I came here," I said. "I wish to speak with you about Miryam."

She smiled faintly. "Yes. Miryam."

"Akiva said you introduced her to him."

"Yes. Half a year ago or so. He is a nice man, Akiva. I wanted her to know him and to have a look around his place."

"So she could get clients there?"

"Yes. It's a good place for that." Her face shifted, turning more serious than it had been till now. "Akiva said you were looking for her."

"Yes."

"For Miryam. On behalf of her family."

"Yes."

"You lie."

"Why would you say that?"

"Because then you'd know her real name."

I said nothing for a moment. I had not expected Sima Vaaknin to know Maryam's true identity.

"Her real name is Maryam Jamalka," I said.

Sima nodded her head an inch or so in acknowledgment. "Why the lie?"

"That's the name she gave Akiva and Lydia. I figured it was the name she'd given you. Or was it the name you gave her instead?"

She smiled. "Maryam and Miryam. Almost the same, yet one is Arab, the other Hebrew. If she wanted to work in Tel Aviv, the Hebrew name would serve her much better. I told her she could pretend to be like me—a Moroccan Jew. It explained her accent. Okay, so you know who she really is. But you are still not being truthful. Akiva got the impression that Maryam's family had sent you to find her, to see if she's well. But Maryam's family would not do that. They may try to find her, but not to see how she was doing."

"She told you about her family?"

"She told me everything," Sima said simply, like a woman who was used to hearing secrets. And I could believe that she was. Whether across a pillow or in her living room, like sunshine on flower petals, she could open people up.

"She was frightened of her family?"

"Yes. And with good reason."

"Even her brother Ahmed?"

Sima tilted her head, pursing her lips in a way that made them look fuller, riper, ready to be kissed. "No. Not him. He wouldn't harm her, but he would also not help her. He's the obedient sort. He wants to look good in his father's eyes."

"When was the last time you saw Maryam?"

"Three months ago."

"Why so long ago?"

She waved her hand. "You still haven't told me why you're here. You'd better hurry, our time is short. I work later this evening."

An image of her nude and in lovemaking flashed across my mind. Across from me, her eyes narrowed in amusement. I mentally waved the image aside, shifting in my seat once more, and tried to focus on what I was there to uncover. I had come here planning to keep the fate of Maryam Jamalka a secret, as I had done with Akiva and Lydia. But Sima Vaaknin was reading every expression on my face. I doubted I could hide the truth from her for much longer. Especially if I wanted her to tell me what she knew.

"Maryam is dead," I said.

There was only a slight shift in her face, a twitch of her lips, a flicker in her eyes. Her breath deepened for two inhalations and exhalations. She looked composed, but the amusement was gone. I suddenly realized that at some point in her life, Sima Vaaknin had known a great deal of sorrow. Only people with an experience of deep grief and private coping could handle bad news with such equanimity.

"How did she die?" Sima asked.

"She was murdered."

"How?"

"A knife. Someone stabbed her. A month ago."

She said nothing.

"Did you try to find her during the past three months to see how she was doing?"

"No," she said simply, and did not elaborate or explain. "Why did you lie? Why pretend she is alive?"

"Not a lot of people know she is dead. It would make my job easier if this remains the case. I'm trying to find out who killed her."

"Why? What was she to you?"

"Her brother asked me to. Ahmed."

"Yes. Ahmed. It figures."

Her tone had gone flat, emotionless. She looked distant. Beautiful and desirable, but not fully present.

"How did you know Maryam? How did you two meet?"

"I found her," she said.

"Found her?"

"In the south of the city, close to the bus terminal. I was out shopping for clothes or just enjoying the sun, I don't remember which. It was shortly before noon, I remember that. A gorgeous, sunny day. I love the sun. I was walking and I saw her sitting on a bench, crying. So I stopped by to see what was the matter with her."

"And what did she say?"

"At first she said nothing. She wouldn't even tell me her name. Said she was fine. I could tell she was an Arab. I said something to her in Arabic, and that opened her up. She told me she was waiting for a man, her lover. She said she'd been in Tel Aviv for four days, and each day she came to the bus terminal to wait for her lover, who was supposed to come meet her there. At night she would sleep at some fleabag hotel in Jaffa. And in the morning she would pack up her things into a small backpack and take up her vigil by the bus terminal."

"And the lover didn't show."

"Which was why she was crying. She was alone and gradually coming to terms with the fact that he was not coming. So she cried."

"And what did you do?"

"I told her to get up and come with me. I brought her here."

"To this apartment?"

She nodded. "I have a spare room. I let her sleep here. It was nice. Like having a sister again."

I wondered what had happened to Sima Vaaknin's real sister, but I didn't ask.

"And then she became a call girl, like you."

Sima arched her left eyebrow a bit, as though affronted by the suggestion that any other woman could be like her.

"No," she said. "At least not straight away. Maryam was a romantic, a hopeless one. You see, despite her lover not showing up when he was supposed to, she was still hoping he would come. She told me about him, how handsome he was, how he said he loved her, that they planned to get married despite the objections of her family. I could tell he had been using her. Some women are blind to the lies men tell, but not me. I told her she was waiting in vain, but she wouldn't listen. She was in love. And women who are in love do not become prostitutes."

"What made her change her mind?"

"She learned he was dead. That he had been killed."

"Did she know who killed him?"

"Her brothers. Not Ahmed. The other two."

"Jalal and Kadir," I said.

"Yes. Those two."

"Was she afraid they would come after her next?"

"Yes. She was always afraid of that. But now she was more angry at them than scared of them. She wanted revenge. And she got it, in a slightly twisted way."

"By becoming a prostitute?"

"Yes." Sima smiled. "You see, they killed her lover because their romance had tarnished the name of her family. Their honor. But that was nothing in comparison to having their sister become a prostitute."

"Wouldn't they need to know what she was doing to care about it?"

"Not in Maryam's mind. It was revenge enough that she knew."

"So you showed her the ropes."

"I taught her how to dress, how to approach men, and better yet, how to make them approach her. I told her what to be careful of."

"And she started working?"

"Yes."

"And how did it go?"

"Have you seen a picture of Maryam?"

I showed her the head shot Ahmed Jamalka had given me.

Sima took it from me, her fingertip brushing along my fingers. She looked at it for a moment, then handed it back.

"She was a beautiful girl. More than the picture shows. There was something naive about her that men liked. She did not have trouble finding clients."

"She brought them here?"

"No. I live here. No one works here but me. I helped Maryam find a place of her own. Even paid the rent for the first month. But I told her not to take them there. Not to a rented apartment. There are some hotels you can go to. I think she used one that isn't far from Akiva's place."

I asked for the address where Maryam Jamalka had lived and wrote it down in my notebook. "Do you have any idea who might have killed her?"

"No. But I can take a guess."

"You think her brothers did it."

"Don't you?"

I didn't tell her about Ahmed Jamalka being sure his brothers did not kill Maryam. Instead I asked, "Why did you take her in? Weren't you afraid of her brothers?

"I was repaying an old debt," Sima said, and she got a faraway look in her eyes, and her hands tightened into small fists on her thighs before opening again.

"A debt? To Maryam Jamalka?"

"No. I never met her before that day by the bus terminal."

When she didn't elaborate, I decided to let it go. Sima Vaaknin could read the lies and uncover the secrets of others, and she was also very good at keeping her own secrets to herself.

"You said you haven't seen Maryam for three months. Why? What happened?"

Sima's face darkened, her jaw tightened, and her lips pinched together. It was a bigger reaction than the one she'd shown when I told her that Maryam Jamalka was dead. "She broke the first and foremost rule of being a prostitute."

"What did she do?"

"She got herself a pimp."

She uttered the word *pimp* as if her tongue rebelled at it, like she was trying to spit out a rotten morsel of sticky food.

"She didn't see him for what he was," Sima said. "As I said, she was a romantic. She fell in love again. The way she saw it, he was her man, her lover, not her pimp. But the moment she told me she'd met someone, someone she slept with on the job, I got suspicious. As a general rule, men don't become involved with prostitutes. I asked her if she gave him some of the money she earned, and she said she was happy to give it to him, that it was an act of love. She said he got clients for her, but that didn't mean he was her pimp either."

"And it made you mad?" I said.

"I don't allow pimps anywhere near me. They always try to control more women. I am free. No one controls me. Once she had a pimp, she was out of my life."

"Did he ever beat her?"

"I don't know. Some pimps do, but only the stupid ones. Girls with bruises are less attractive to clients."

"Do you know the name of the pimp?"

She shook her head. "I never met him, and Maryam never told me his name. The moment I knew she had a pimp I told her to stay away from me and not to call me while she was still with him."

"Was there anyone else, from before you two lost contact, who was fixated on her, who threatened her in any way?"

"She never told me of anyone. I warned her of such men and told her to tell me if she met one."

I could think of nothing more to ask. Perhaps later, once I allowed my mind the time and freedom to go over my conversation with Sima Vaaknin, something would come up that would need clarification. But for now...

She was looking at me. The darkness had left her face, and

her lips and jaw had relaxed. The glint of amusement had returned to her eyes.

"You have run out of questions," she said.

"Yes."

"But you are not saying goodbye."

"No."

"You want to stay," she said. It was not a question.

I couldn't say yes, and I couldn't say no. Both were true. I wanted her with an eagerness that was unexpected, the sort of craving I hadn't felt for years. But I was also wary. I sensed that being with her would take me deeper than I dared go.

My mouth suddenly turned dry, and my palms became damp with prickly sweat. I kept silent.

She turned her head to look at a clock that stood on a side table. "There is not enough time," she said. "You may think it won't take long, but it will. I will make sure of it."

She smiled at me, a seductress reveling in her powers. "You ask too many questions, Adam Lapid. So many questions."

"It's what I do," I managed to say.

"Perhaps if you come by on another night, you will do a bit more. After ten. Then we won't need to hurry."

It was a cue. I had to leave. I figured she was expecting a man, a client. Someone who would soon occupy the place that I had been offered for a future night, who would occupy her.

I rose from my chair, with my hands fisted by my thighs and a strange current thrumming through my arms. If her client had knocked on her door at that moment, I would have punched him hard enough to bust his jaw.

When I turned my back to her, I realized that I had been holding my breath. I was keenly aware of her presence as she saw me to the door.

I reached for the handle, drew the door open, and was about

to step out when she said, "Tell your client that his sister loved him."

I turned. The amusement was gone from her face, but it had not been replaced by sadness. If there was anything to be read in her eyes and the set of her features, I couldn't say what it was.

"Despite the fact that he abandoned her," she said. "That was Maryam. A hopeless romantic."

# 13

It was not yet six when I exited Sima Vaaknin's building. A fast wind was whipping down the street like the excited gasp of approaching winter beginning to assert itself. I took a few deep breaths. I had not reacted to a woman this way since my wife died. Perhaps, and I was not sure I cared to admit it, I had not reacted the same way to my wife when she was alive.

I had loved my Deborah. I still did, despite the five years that had passed since her death in Auschwitz. But my attraction to her came from a different place than what I had felt for Sima Vaaknin. It was a more cerebral and emotional sort of attraction, and with Sima it stemmed from a baser instinct.

Earlier that day it had been hot, and I hadn't taken my jacket with me. Now I wished I had it on, for the wind had brought cold with it. I got a pack of cigarettes out of my pants pocket, tapped one out, and stuck it in my mouth. It took three matches to light it; the wind kept blowing them out. I stood for a moment, taking smoke in and letting it out. The wind carried the smoke away along with a scattering of leaves and a balled-up newspaper. A man was walking toward me on the sidewalk. He was in his early forties, just under six feet in height, with black hair that had started to recede, and a lean frame without a lot of muscle on his bones. He was wearing a gray suit with a white shirt and a black tie. He held a brown leather briefcase in his left hand. His shoes made tapping sounds on the pavement. As he approached, I kept my eyes on him. He caught my gaze, frowned, gradually slowed his step and came to a halt about fifteen feet from where I stood. With a wary expression on his face, he crossed to the other side of the street and walked quickly away.

I let out a shaky breath. I had thought he might be Sima's next client, and I had wanted to...what? Not to confront him, surely? What was there to confront him about?

I didn't know what I had planned on doing, and I didn't want to find out. I walked quickly in the opposite direction with my head down and caught the first bus that came along.

I got off on the northern tip of King George Street and dropped onto a bench at Masaryk Square. I smoked another cigarette, letting the smoke pass into me and the time pass on by me. I thought about my dead wife, Deborah, seeing her face vividly in my mind. I saw her laughing and thought I could hear a faint echo of her laughter. Then I heard her weeping, and that sound was as clear as the report of a gun. I felt guilty, as if I had betrayed her.

When my cigarette was done, I began walking south, taking a left to Zamenhof Street, and continued onward to Dizengoff Square. The square was the center of the heart of Tel Aviv and teemed with people. There were those who passed through on their way home from work, and others who stopped by for a coffee or a chat with friends. I wended my way through the crowds and got off the square to Pinsker Street. I took a right to Trumpeldor Street, passing the cemetery to my right. Through the open gate, I caught a glimpse of the mismatched headstones of the early residents of Tel Aviv, some ornate and imposing, others simple and of modest girth and height. I pondered the death of Maryam Jamalka. How had she been memorialized? What did her burial place look like? Did anyone visit it apart from her brother, Ahmed, or was it considered best avoided and forgotten, a taboo like what she had become?

I entered Hovevei Tsiyon Street and stopped before the three-story structure where Maryam Jamalka had lived. The building was square and narrow, with clean straight lines and medium-sized balconies. The front yard sported a number of carefully maintained shrubs and short trees, and the flagstone walkway to the front door had been recently swept clean. Maryam's apartment was on the third floor and faced the street. I looked at her window from below, and there was no sign of movement within. The entrance hall was clean and cool. I checked the mailboxes and couldn't find Miryam Cohen, the name Maryam Jamalka went by. The mailbox for her apartment was labeled Roy and Yafa Altbauer.

I walked up the stairs and knocked on the door marked Altbauer. The sound reverberated in the stairwell and small landing before being swallowed by the emptiness of her apartment. I put my nose to the door but could detect no bad odor, or any other scent, wafting from within.

A door opened to my left, and a young pear-shaped woman with auburn hair stood in the doorway.

"Oh," she said, "I thought you were Miryam."

She was wearing a loose white shirt with its hem tucked into the waistline of a plaid skirt. The skirt went to her knees, and below them her legs were encased in brown stockings. She had an open face with a prominent nose and kind brown eyes. An engagement ring glinted on her left hand.

"Sorry to disappoint," I said, deciding to resume hiding the fact that Maryam was dead. "Were you expecting her?"

"Well, no. In fact, I have no reason to expect her to come back. Mr. Gordon said she'd left, and someone else is living in her apartment now. But she didn't say goodbye, and anytime I hear strange footsteps on the landing, I start hoping—"

"Who is Mr. Gordon?" I asked.

"The landlord."

"Does he live here?"

"Downstairs. Ground floor."

"When did Miryam leave?"

"Has something happened to her? Who are you?"

I realized that I was coming on too strong, asking questions like a policeman interviewing a suspect. If I was going to get answers, I would need to employ a softer approach.

I introduced myself, and she told me her name was Sarit Gruber.

I said, "I'm looking for Miryam. I know that she lived here. When was the last time you saw her?"

"Two and a half months ago. Maybe a bit longer."

"Were you friends?"

She appeared to give this some thought. "I liked her, but I can't say for sure how she felt about me. We were friendly. I invited her to join us a few times when I had friends over, but she only came once and never again."

"Did she say why?"

"No. But when I look back I think it had to do with a friend of my fiancé—he wasn't my fiancé at the time, just my suitor—who took an interest in her. He asked me to talk with her, see if she was available, and she said she wasn't. But I never saw a suitor come calling for her."

I could imagine what happened. Maryam Jamalka, new to living a lie, was approached by a nice Jewish man looking for romance. What could she do? Build another floor or two on the building of lies that was her life? Engage him as a lover? Try to recruit him as a client? Either was risky and likely went against the lessons imparted by Sima Vaaknin. This apartment and her work were to remain separated.

"Do you live here alone?" I asked.

"No," she said. "I live with another girl. I can't afford this place by myself."

"Was your roommate also on friendly terms with Miryam?"

"Daniella never met her. She just moved in here a month ago. My previous roommate got married and moved all the way to Eilat. But she didn't like Miryam very much. I remember her saying that there was something strange about Miryam, but she couldn't pinpoint it."

"Was there something strange about her?" I asked.

She thought for a moment before answering. "She was obviously new to Tel Aviv, and she often stayed out very late at night. My roommate said she was loose. With men, I mean. But I don't know that it's true."

"And what was Miryam's mood like when she lived here?"

"What do you mean?"

"Was she happy?"

"I think so. She always smiled at me when we ran into each other. But I couldn't say for certain. She mostly kept to herself. Was quiet. I never even heard music coming from her place." She grinned. "Me, I had to be told twice by Mr. Gordon to keep the volume down. One of the neighbors below is a bit older, and the noise gets him riled up."

"And the other neighbor?" I asked.

She laughed. "She's also old, but the music doesn't bother her because she's going deaf." She grew serious. "I shouldn't have said that. It wasn't nice. As for Miryam, come to think of it, I know very little about her. She told me she worked as a secretary in some business in the south of the city, but I can't recall the name of the business or what they do. I don't know whether she has any brothers and sisters. I don't know where she came from. I must have asked, but she never told me. It's funny. You live next door to a person for months and you hardly know them."

Like the third floor, the second floor housed two apartments, and I knocked on the doors of both. In one lived a couple in their fifties, the Shalits. When I asked about their neighbor, remembering to call her Miryam Cohen, both knew who I was referring to, but neither could offer any detail that illuminated her life, and certainly not her death.

In the other apartment, an elderly woman with thick glasses peered up at me. She spoke in the loud, unconscious voice of those whose hearing was failing. I asked her about Miryam Cohen, and she told me that once, must have been less than three months ago, when she was returning from her shopping, the "nice young woman," as she called her, took her bags from her and carried them upstairs to the old woman's apartment, arranging them in her kitchen.

"She told me she would be happy to carry them for me anytime I went shopping, but I told her that wouldn't be necessary. I look frail, but I still got some strength in my bones. And besides, she was such a lovely young thing. She should not waste her time on an old woman like me. She should enjoy her youth."

As for any visitors the young woman might have had, she couldn't say. She never ventured up to the third floor, and her hearing was not what it used to be.

"You get to a point where most of the things you hear are those you've heard before," she told me. "You see a bus go by and your mind supplies the sound it is supposed to make. A child laughs and you hear the laughter of your own child at that age. But new sounds and the things you cannot see, those you remain ignorant of."

Mr. Gordon, the landlord, was in his early fifties and had the hard body of a man who had done his share of manual labor. He was wearing a white undershirt that showed off muscular arms with skin that age was beginning to loosen. His wide shoulders and broad chest were covered with coarse curls of black and gray hair. His face was tanned, and lines webbed the corners of his hazel eyes. He was losing his hair and had it cropped close to his scalp. On his left wrist was a watch with a broad leather band and a large display. He was as tall as I was, and his handshake was strong.

He invited me in, and we sat in his sparsely appointed living room. He offered me a beer and took one for himself.

I asked him about Miryam Cohen.

"Left two and a half months ago," he said. "Totally caught me by surprise. Just came to my door one day and told me she was leaving."

"She didn't say why?"

His face creased in disgust. "No, but she didn't need to. It was a man. I've seen him around. Slimy little fellow. Half a head shorter than you and I, black hair, weak looking. Don't know what she saw in him. A beautiful girl, that one."

"He used to come around to her apartment?"

"Saw him twice, maybe three times around here. Didn't like him the instant I saw him. Slimy. The kind that tries to get by with as little work as possible. Shortly after I saw him the first time, she told me she was leaving. I kept the apartment for her for another six weeks, hoping she'd see the light, lose the guy, and come back. But she didn't. Finally rented out the apartment. A nice couple lives there now."

"Do you know the name of the man?"

"Never talked to him."

"Anything special about his face? Any identifying features?"

"He had close-set eyes. Small ones. Dark in color. And his skin was dark. Darker than Miryam's."

"No beard or mustache?"

"No." He took down half the beer in his glass in one big gulp, looked at me with a frown and said, "Who hired you to look for her, the sister?"

"Sister?" I asked.

"The one who came with her the first time. Paid the rent for the first month." He went on to describe the sister, and I realized he was referring to Sima Vaaknin. I brought up the image of Maryam Jamalka from the picture her brother had given me, juxtaposed it in my mind with my vivid recollection of Sima Vaaknin, and could see why Gordon would mistake them for sisters. There was a resemblance—a similar complexion, about the same hair color, both attractive. Sima had spoken of the time Maryam had stayed with her in her apartment, how it was like having a sister again. Was it her appearance that drove Sima to take her in?

"They're not sisters," I said. "She was a friend."

"Has to be a close friend to pay the rent for her." He looked at me. "You said 'was a friend.' "

"They had a falling out. Hadn't seen each other for a while. I just spoke to her earlier today. Her name is Sima."

"Nice woman," Gordon said, and I gave him a look. But he didn't seem to be having any lewd thoughts.

"Do you know where Miryam moved to?"

He shook his head. "No idea."

"Let me guess, you asked, but she wouldn't say."

He nodded. "Exactly."

"How did she move her stuff? Her furniture?"

"The apartment came furnished. Just basic stuff, nothing fancy. Easier to rent that way with all the new people coming here with hardly no money besides what they make month to month. So all she had to cart away were her clothes and personal items. Wouldn't need a truck for that. A car would do."

"Apart from the man, did she have any visitors?"

"No one I can remember. That doesn't mean much. I don't pry into the life of my tenants. As long as there are no complaints and I don't notice something fishy, I stay out of their lives. You could ask Sarit, her neighbor on the floor."

I told him I had already spoken with her. I drank some of my beer. He drained his glass and went to the kitchen to get himself another.

When he came back, I asked, "What was Miryam like? What was your impression of her?"

He turned the question over in his mind, taking slow, measured sips from his beer.

Then: "She was quiet, polite. In the beginning she would avert her eyes when I saw her in the hall or outside in the street. Maybe she was shy. I don't know. Could never read women that well. I could tell you one thing, though. There were times I got the sense that she was scared of something. Couldn't tell you what it was, if there was anything there at all. But that's what I believe."

I asked Gordon if I could take a look at the apartment. He told me it was up to the current tenants. We climbed the stairs together, and he made the introductions with the black-haired man who answered the door, Roy Altbauer. He said I could come right in, though he couldn't imagine what I would find there.

"There was nothing of her in the apartment when we moved in."

It was a nice apartment, spacious, well lit, clean, with good airflow from several directions. I looked around the kitchen, the bathroom, the bedroom. It wasn't a proper search. I didn't go through the closets, look under the mattress, or check for loose tiles under which something had been stashed. But I sensed that

Altbauer was right. If a piece of Maryam Jamalka had remained behind when she left this apartment, it had long since vanished. A wave of sadness washed over me. I wanted to get a better sense of who she was, how she made this place her home, but there was nothing. Just another part of Maryam Jamalka that had been erased.

# 14

Mr. Gordon and I left Maryam's former apartment and descended the stairs to the ground floor. As I made to leave the building, he said to me, "When you find her, let me know, will you? I'd like to know that she's all right."

I gave a noncommittal nod and walked out to the street. The wind from before had kicked up dust and dirt from the roads and yards and the air smelled dirty and thick.

I walked back to Allenby Street and went into Greta's Café. Sitting at my table, I had two cups of her excellent coffee one right after the other. Outside on the street the last traces of sunlight were evaporating and the eerie fake light of the streetlights came on to do battle with the natural darkness of night. Somewhere close by, a killer was roaming, a man who had taken a knife to a young woman, who'd marked her body for pleasure or to satiate some inner urge or hunger that plagued him. A man who'd left her naked and mutilated body in the Yarkon River. Was I closer to finding this man? Perhaps. I had learned some things about the life Maryam Jamalka had led in Tel Aviv. I knew where she'd stayed and how she'd lived her life up to two months before her body was discovered. I knew she'd experienced kindness and hospitality and friendship. I knew she had lost that friendship by falling in love with the wrong man.

I couldn't help but think that twice in her life, Maryam Jamalka had lost her family because of what Sima Vaaknin called "her hopeless romanticism." The first time she fell in love with a man of the wrong faith and lost her birth family. The second time her lover was a man of the wrong profession, and that cost her a woman who had treated her like a sister. In both cases, the men she'd loved had taken advantage of her. The first of these men was dead. The second was still nameless, his fate unknown. I had to find this second man, this pimp for whom Maryam had lost Sima and given up her apartment on Hovevei Tsiyon Street.

A little after eight, I said goodnight to Greta and exited the café. I walked south, enjoying the cool air, and for a while I let my mind go where it pleased. Thoughts came and went without order or direction, and none stuck or came forward to demand my attention. I walked all the way to Elifelet Street and got to Club Adom at a quarter after nine.

It wasn't as busy as the night before, and the crowd seemed to lean more towards couples than men looking to feast their eyes or other parts of their anatomy on young, purchasable women. I didn't see Lydia, but Akiva was manning the bar, once again sporting a black bow tie.

He smiled when he saw me and began drawing me a beer before I had a chance to ask for one. I laid money on the bar, and he made it disappear.

"Did you meet with Sima?" he asked me.

I nodded and sipped some beer. I kept my eyes on my glass, feeling him peering at me. Finally I looked up and met his eyes. "You're wondering if I slept with her."

Now it was his turn to look down. He cleared his throat and I regretted being so blunt. I was about to say I was sorry when he spoke. "I was wondering if you learned anything about Miryam."

"A little. Sima told me about meeting her and bringing her here." I decided not to say anything about visiting Maryam's old apartment. No use having people from this part of her life snooping around that part. What I said was, "Sima told me that a few months ago, Miryam got seriously involved with someone. A pimp."

Akiva blinked and his eyes narrowed in a frown.

"Do you know anything about that?" I asked.

"No. It's no secret that I don't like pimps, and if I ever found one hanging around here, I would throw him out. The girls know that. But I don't doubt that some of them have boyfriends who are little more than pimps. I can't do anything about what happens outside these walls."

"Do you remember someone sitting around while Miryam was here working? He would have likely sat by himself, not gotten into conversation with any of the girls, including Miryam." Akiva was shaking his head till I mentioned that the guy looked "slimy," which stopped the shaking abruptly and made Akiva's eyes widen.

"There was someone. Thin, dressed in black clothes. Had black hair, combed back and shiny. Probably used Brilliantine or some other similar product. He never sat at the bar, always at a table by the wall. And always alone. That's unusual. Most people come here with company, and those that come alone usually intend on getting company of the paid-for variety."

"Was he ever here on nights when Miryam wasn't?"

Akiva thought it over. "No. I couldn't say so with any certainty, but I think he never was. I hadn't noticed it at the time. I don't recall them coming in together or ever speaking with each other."

"Probably because she knew what you thought of pimps."

"Probably so."

"When did he start coming by here?"

"I couldn't say."

"I don't need an exact date, Akiva. Just an estimate."

Akiva shut his eyes and took a deep breath to help his concentration. "Oh, I'd say three months ago, maybe a couple of weeks earlier than that."

"And the last time you saw him?"

He had been polishing a glass with a rag, and his hands paused as the answer came to him. He looked at me with rounded eyes. "The night she was arrested. I remember that distinctly. He was sitting right there at that table when the policeman handcuffed Miryam. I remember her turning her head in his direction. I couldn't see her expression and she didn't say anything, but she could have been looking right at him. When the policeman led her out, the man quickly followed. He never came back in. Come to think of it, he didn't even settle his tab that night."

"And after Miryam was released, when she came here?"

"I don't remember seeing him again," Akiva said. "I'm pretty sure he never returned."

I drank the rest of my beer while he went to pour drinks and exchange pleasantries with other patrons. It seemed I had uncovered another pivotal moment in the final months of Maryam Jamalka's life. The first was when Sima and she broke contact over the new man in Maryam's life. The second came shortly after, when Maryam gave up her apartment, again because of the man. The third was her arrest. It marked a change in her behavior, and it was the last time her pimp had been seen in Club Adom.

And the arrest itself was unusual. Normally, I had learned from my talk with Lydia, prostitutes were not taken into custody, and they weren't subjected to a three-day stay in jail. They came to some accommodation with the arresting officer and were let go. Why had Maryam's arrest been different?

I had the name of the arresting officer from the crime report Yossi Talmon had given me. I could go talk to him or ask Reuben to sniff around for me. Either approach was problematic. If I talked to the arresting officer, it might make it to Inspector Rosen's ears, and so far I'd been able to avoid coming to his attention. And as for Reuben, I did not want to involve him any deeper in this case. Not unless I had to.

For now, I was still making progress on my own. I would reconsider my options if and when I hit a dead end.

When Akiva finished with the other customers and came back to stand across the bar from me, I asked him if Lydia might know who the man was, and he said that she might.

"Has she been around tonight?" I asked.

"Not yet. She isn't here every night, but she might still show up."

He wrinkled his face when I asked him about the hotel that the prostitutes took men to.

"It's a sleazy place. Wouldn't sleep there if you paid me."

"Do you have the address?"

He did and he wrote it down for me. He gave me a long look as he handed me the paper. "Ever since our talk the night before, I've been thinking."

"What about?"

"About Miryam and her not coming around here no more, and you asking all these questions. Should I be worried about her?"

"No," I said, and it was the truth, but not the way he meant it. Worrying about Maryam Jamalka, or Miryam Cohen, as he thought of her, was pointless. She was beyond worry or help.

"Somehow that doesn't convince me. I keep thinking she might be in trouble somehow, or..." His face turned pale and he swallowed so hard his Adam's apple wobbled like a buoy in a stormy sea. "I can't bring myself to say it."

"So don't," I said. "Don't say it."

He rubbed his mouth and cheeks. "Why not? Do you think it will change anything? Like the evil eye or something?"

"No," I said. "Words change nothing. Bad things happen with or without them. But if they make you feel bad or sad or sick to your stomach, then don't say them."

He nodded shakily. "All right. I won't."

At that moment Lydia walked in. She tottered a bit, steadying herself on the back of a chair. She was wearing a clinging black skirt that stopped above her knees and a low-cut white blouse that showed a portion of her breasts. She came over to the bar and leaned on it in a way that brought emphasis to her bust. She smelled of cigarettes and alcohol and an underlying scent of recent sexual contact. She flashed me a lascivious smile. "You've changed your mind? You're here for me?"

"No. Just asking some more questions."

She rolled her eyes. "You with your questions. Are you just cold, or do you have nothing left in you after Sima?"

"Lydia," Akiva said in a voice part admonishing and part beseeching.

She spread her arms in a show of innocence. "What? What did I say? Get me a drink, will you, Akiva?"

"How many did you have so far tonight?" I asked.

She turned on me, her face red. "What do you care? You're not my father nor my husband. You don't even want to be my client. But that doesn't matter. There are plenty of men who are eager for my company."

"Maybe Adam is right," Akiva said.

"Adam doesn't know anything," she shot back. "That's right, isn't it?" she said to me. "You don't know anything. That's why you're here asking all these questions."

"Maybe you can help me with that. I understand that Miryam began seeing a man three months ago." I described him to her. "Do you remember him?"

"There was someone like that," she said after a moment. "I saw him around with her outside once, and she tried to introduce us, but I said I was in a hurry. I never saw him with her again."

"Did you know he was her pimp?" I asked.

"No. She never told me she had a pimp."

"Do you remember his name?"

She scrunched up her face, her cheeks flushed with alcohol. "Something foreign."

"Foreign how? Russian, German, American, Arab?"

"Not Russian," she said, rubbing her temple. "American, I think. I'm not sure. What difference does it make?"

"Try to remember," I said. "It's important."

"What's important is that I get something to drink. Enough with your questions already. Get me a drink, Akiva. I need it. I don't want to make a scene."

It was a little late for that, as some of the other patrons were giving us uncomfortable looks. Akiva must have noticed them, too, because he sighed and poured her a shot.

"Last one, all right?"

"Yeah, yeah," she said, gulping down the drink. She looked at me, and her eyes were bleary with alcohol. "I don't remember his name, okay? I see plenty of men. They all get mixed up in my mind after a while."

With that she staggered off toward a table where two young men were sitting. They smiled when she approached, and one of them lit her cigarette for her.

"Does she always drink like this?" I asked.

"Often, I'm afraid."

"What's her story?"

"Her story?"

"Why did she become a prostitute? She said she had a husband."

Akiva grimaced. "Yes. But he's no catch. He's a bum and more of a drunk than her. They have two children. Twin girls, two years old. He doesn't work, so she has to feed them all by herself. She can make more money by sleeping with men than with any other job she's likely to get. And she gets to spend the day with her girls. I hate to think what will happen when they grow up enough to understand how she makes her living."

"Maybe they'll appreciate the sacrifices she made for them," I said.

"Maybe. Or maybe they'll be ashamed of her. And maybe Lydia will be too drunk to care either way."

I finished my beer and shook my head no when he offered to fill up my glass for me.

"And what about Sima? What is her story?"

Akiva smiled faintly. "She got to you, didn't she?"

I said nothing, and a silent moment stretched between us. Then, for no reason I could fathom, I said, "I didn't sleep with her," and felt foolish for having said it.

"I didn't say you did," Akiva said, and I appreciated it when his faint smile did not broaden. "I don't know her story. I've known Sima Vaaknin for a few years, but I have no idea where she came from, whether she has any parents or siblings, or what her life was like before. I don't even know if she enjoys what she does or if it's just something she's good at. That's the only thing I know for sure, that she's good at what she does."

And that she was kind to Maryam Jamalka, I thought to myself.

I left Club Adom and made my way to Alfasi Street, where the hotel Akiva had described as "sleazy" was located. It was a five-minute walk, and I could well understand its appeal as a place of operation for the working girls who picked up their johns at Club Adom.

A small sign above the front door announced that I was standing in front of the Jaffa Star Hotel. It was a three-story structure with a rough-hewn dirty stone exterior and long and narrow round-top windows along its front. There were no balconies, which was appropriate since most of the guests spent no more than an hour or so in their rooms.

The lights were on in a few of the rooms, but dark curtains were drawn across all the windows. The front door was held open by a gray brick, and the lobby beyond it was small and devoid of any furniture, paintings, or plants. Just stone walls that could use a new layer of paint and a counter at the far end, where an overweight man sat in his undershirt.

His cheeks were marked by a few days' worth of stubble, and his scalp looked oily past his thinning dark-brown hair. There was a half-eaten sandwich on the counter and two newspapers spread beside it, partially illuminated by a weak lamp whose light was further muffled by its dusty yellow lampshade.

The man watched me approach without a change in his expression and did not offer any greeting when I stopped across the counter.

"What can I do for you?" he asked. His voice was gruff and bored.

"You the manager?"

"I own the place," he said. "You want a room? Or just someone to keep you company for a while?"

He leered at me, exposing uneven teeth. I shook my head.

"Neither," I said, "I want information about a woman who used to frequent this hotel." I took out Maryam's head shot and laid it on the counter. "This one."

His leer was replaced by wariness. He said, "Never seen her in my life."

"You've got special eyes, anyone ever tell you that?"

"What are you talking about?"

"You could tell you never saw her without even glancing at her picture. That's a neat trick."

He narrowed his eyes at me, the fat in his cheeks bunching up like rolled-up dough. "You with the police?"

"Just look at the picture."

"If you're not with the police, I don't have to do what you want. In fact, why don't you get the hell out of here and leave me in peace?"

"Look at the picture and give me an answer, and then I'll leave."

"Don't feel like it." He smirked at me and reached a fat hand toward the remains of his sandwich. I slammed my hand down hard on his, trapping it against the hard surface of the counter. He let out a cry of pain and tried withdrawing his hand, but I pushed down, putting my arm and shoulder into it, crushing his fingers.

His face turned red and he twisted in his seat so hard it toppled over. He nearly fell, which put even more tension on his trapped hand, and he let out a bellow like someone had stuck a knife in his stomach. Gasping for air, he pushed himself up with his free hand.

"Let go," he wheezed.

I shook my head. "Look at the damn picture."

"Okay. Okay." He picked up the picture and held it in front of his face. "Don't know her. Satisfied? Now let go of me."

"No," I said. "I know she used this hotel. A lot of prostitutes do. Keep lying and you won't be able to use this hand for a month." I applied a little more pressure.

"Dammit! Okay, I've seen her around. But not lately. Name was Miri or Mor or Miryam. Something like that."

I kept my hold on him and started to ask him about

Maryam's pimp, when the door in the wall behind the counter opened and a young, lanky man stuck his head out.

He had big bulging eyes, a sallow complexion, and cheeks scored with acne. His hair was dirty blond and limp. He was holding a large wrench.

"What's going on here?"

I let go of the manager and he backed up as far as he could go, rubbing his damaged hand with the other.

"What took you so long?" the manager said to the young man. "This maniac nearly broke my hand. Didn't you hear me scream?"

"I was fixing a pipe downstairs when I heard something. I came up as fast as I could."

I held up Maryam's picture. "This woman. I'm looking for a guy who used to hang around her. A pimp."

"Go to hell. We're not answering any of your questions."

The young man said nothing, but I could see recognition in his eyes. He also remembered Maryam.

"Shorter than me," I said. "Black hair. Small eyes. No beard. No mustache. Slimy looking."

The manager's face was like a tomato, anger and humiliation making his blood vessels expand. He started shouting at me to get out when his eyes darted over my shoulder, and whatever he was about to scream died in his throat.

I half-turned and saw a man and a woman enter the lobby. The woman was young and thin and blond. The man was pudgy and in his early forties. She was wearing a black dress and high heels. He was dressed in a gray suit and a blue tie. He looked drunk and had a stupid smile on his face. She looked businesslike and serious. If they noticed us at all, they gave no sign of it. She led him by the hand across the lobby straight to the staircase. The clicking of her heels on the exposed stone gradually diminished till they couldn't be heard at all.

"I'm willing to pay for the information," I said.

"We're telling you nothing," the manager said. "And if you don't get out of here, I'll call the police. I have friends there, and they'll be glad to work on you some." He reached for an off-white telephone on the counter, and I put Maryam's photo back in my pocket, turned around and walked away. He yelled curses and threats at me till I stepped out into the street.

Outside, the night was quiet and the street empty. I put my hand in my pocket as I walked, rummaging for my almost depleted pack of cigarettes. I had one out when I noticed a tall, thin figure approaching from fifty meters away. He passed under a streetlight, and I saw it was the lanky guy with the wrench from the hotel, the one who had come to the manager's rescue.

At first I thought he was there to fight me, and I tossed my unlit cigarette away and got ready to do battle with my fists, having failed to bring my knife. Then I saw that his hands were empty, and he was holding them palms out and fingers splayed, letting me know that he was weaponless.

He came to a stop ten feet away, shifted on his feet, and said, "I know who her pimp was."

"What's his name?"

He shook his head and gave me a sly smile. "The money first."

I handed over some bills. He wanted a little more, and I was in no mood to argue. I wanted the name of the pimp. Without it, I might never know who killed Maryam Jamalka. I handed over the rest of the money.

"The name," I said.

He told me. I knew that name. Knew it and should have guessed it myself. I wanted to curse and punch and kick that son of a bitch till he couldn't draw breath enough to ask me to stop. But I kept calm and showed the lanky man from the hotel nothing.

"Go back to the hotel," I said, "before the fat guy notices you're gone."

He grinned. "He won't. He went upstairs with one of the girls. That's the only good thing about the job, you know. The girls. They're nice."

His grin got wider, exposing his gums, and my fingers twitched, urging me to curl them into fists. I stretched them out along my thighs. To the man I said, "Go on now."

He turned and went back to whatever back door he'd used to get in front of me on the street. I started to head south but then remembered I didn't have my knife with me. This wouldn't do. When I went to have a chat with Charlie Buzaglo about him being Maryam Jamalka's pimp, I wanted to be armed.

———

At home I got into the shower and let the spray pelt me for a while. Eventually I soaped up, rinsed myself, toweled dry and put on clean shorts and a shirt. I made myself a cup of tea and added a liberal amount of sugar. I sat on the edge of my mattress, holding the cup in both hands, taking the occasional sip.

Charlie Buzaglo. The rat-faced low-life smuggler whom I had seen just the other day with a young girl at his side. Another young prostitute, probably, one to fill the vacancy created by Maryam Jamalka's death. Slimy was the word Mr. Gordon had used to describe the man for whom Maryam Jamalka had given up her apartment, and the word fit Charlie Buzaglo like a glove. And the foreign name—American, Lydia had said. His first name sounded American. That made me smile. Charlie Buzaglo was as far from an American as I was from a Chinese.

I finished my tea and brushed my teeth before realizing that I craved a cigarette. I took it out of the pack, looked at it, and pushed it back in. I lay in bed, staring at the dark-shrouded ceiling with the jutting outline of the bare bulb.

My mind turned to Ahmed Jamalka and Sima Vaaknin. Both had lost a sister. And more than once. Ahmed lost Maryam the first time when she ran away from home and he did nothing to help her. He lost her a second time when she died. Sima had lost a sister somewhere in her past. And she lost another sister when Maryam had committed the cardinal sin of the call girl and got herself a pimp. At first I thought that Sima had been too harsh, but now that I knew the identity of the pimp, I revised my judgment.

I thought of my four sisters, all gone in the gas chambers or due to the wretched conditions of the camps. I was the eldest sibling, the only son. Blanka was the oldest daughter. She'd been twenty-five when we were put on the train to Poland. She had one child, a three-year-old named Gabor. He was probably gassed on arrival, as nearly all young children were. Blanka had suffered three miscarriages and had once told my mother she thought she'd been cursed. Maybe when she was on the train, she'd changed her mind. It must have been easier to comfort a single son during that horrific train ride than three or four.

Sofia was twenty-one and had just gotten married seven months before the expulsion of the Jews of Hungary. It had been a simple ceremony. Very little to eat, very little to drink, but a happy day all the same. She'd been pregnant when she died. Her husband had survived. I'd met him in a camp for the displaced after the war. He'd elected to return to Hungary.

Sarlota was seventeen. Tall and willowy. Her face was the most similar to mine. She was quick to laughter, and to anger as well. She used to sing when she worked around the house. Songs in Hungarian and Hebrew. She had belonged to a local Zionist youth group and had wanted to immigrate to the Land of Israel since she was fifteen. I remembered how she had badgered my mother for permission to go. She'd wanted to join a kibbutz, to raise chickens and crops under the hot sun, to never be hated by her neighbors for being a Jew. But my mother had refused, and Sarlota had fought and argued, but never disobeyed.

The last was Julia, who was only fourteen. Her eyesight was bad, and I recalled taking her to buy eyeglasses in Budapest. She had blue eyes like my mother's. She also had her nose and jawline and had learned to emulate Mother's frowns. I had been thirteen when she was born, right after I'd had my Bar Mitzvah. I remembered my father putting his arm around my shoulder and drawing me aside, talking to me in an earnest voice, telling me that now that I was a man, I had to take care of my baby sister, of all my sisters, and my mother, as well. He had been sick for some months. And I later realized he had known his days were numbered. His trust in me was misplaced. I did not stop the murder of my sisters and mother. Nor did I save my wife and two daughters. Everyone was killed but me.

I ran a hand over my face and scalp and nape. My heart was pounding, and every hair on my arms stood up. I gritted my teeth and tried to erect a wall in my mind to keep the memories at bay. It was too late, I knew. Tonight would be a bad one. I would close my eyes and see. My dreams would bring me my sisters, and they would not be pleasant dreams of childhood memories and family gatherings. They would be dreams of death and fire and suffering. They would be dreams of guilt and heartrending grief. They would be wicked visions of gas chambers, barbed-wire fences, snarling dogs and guard towers. They would keep my sleep brittle. They would make me scream.

I closed my eyes, drew the thin blanket to my chin, and made myself ready for the assault of my dreams.

# 15

When I woke up, I was groggy and had a bad taste in my mouth. My tongue felt swollen. I must have been grinding my teeth since my jaw ached. My body throbbed all over and my muscles felt tight. I could not recall my dreams, but they had not allowed my body any relaxation during the night.

I threw open the window. Below a car horn honked and a woman shouted at her husband that he'd forgotten the keys to his office. A kid was running on the opposite sidewalk, his schoolbag bouncing on his back. The murmur of a radio anchor wafted to my window from a neighboring apartment. Exhaust fumes were coming up from an idling car below, probably the same one whose horn had blared. A moment later I heard a car door slam and its engine rev as it drove away.

I stood at the window, breathing in the morning air, fumes and all, while my head slowly cleared itself of the shadowy remnants of my dreams. Some people forgot their dreams entirely within minutes of waking up. My dreams tended to linger in my mind, especially the bad ones.

Once my mind was clear, I put on some coffee and toasted a

few pieces of bread in a pan. I smeared cheese on the toast. The cheese was also rationed. The guy I used to buy extra from had recently announced that he was getting out of the black market business, so I had but a small supply left and I spread it thin on the bread. It was an okay breakfast. I had had much worse and, on many occasions, had none at all.

After breakfast I sat at my table and read a bit from my book. The hero of the story was a gunfighter who had joined up with a poor farmer whose land was coveted by a big-time rancher of dubious morals and deficient conscience. The story was nothing special—some gunfights, a lot of horseback riding, long and detailed descriptions of scenery, but it was still an enjoyable read. I read for a little over an hour, then marked my place, slipped the book in my pocket, and headed out.

I went to Levinson Drugstore and asked if I had any messages. There was one from Reuben, asking me to call him back. I did, but he wasn't at his desk. I left a message saying I'd try him later. I headed to Greta's and passed the time till noon playing chess and alternately reading the newspaper and the Western I'd started earlier.

Somewhere around two o'clock, just as the hero of the story had entered a saloon full of wicked men who worked for his adversary, a policeman entered Greta's Café. His eyes went about the room and settled on me. He didn't ask if he could join me or wait for me to invite him to sit, but dropped into a chair and gazed at me across the table.

He was of average height, narrow waisted and broad shoul-dered, and handsome in a rigid, masculine sort of way. Mid-thir-ties, with deep gray eyes and a fair complexion. An air of neatness and order about him. Reddish-brown hair, parted neatly along one side. Sideburns as precise and straight as if he had trimmed them that morning with a ruler. He had a wide, square-jawed face dominated by a prominent Roman nose. Between said nose and his thin-lipped mouth, a thick mustache stretched. The mustache was of a darker hue than his hair and looked as meticulously maintained as his hair and sideburns.

I had watched him as he approached. He walked with his shoulders back and his chest pushed out. It was the walk of a soldier, not one marching to battle, but one on parade. His shoes were polished to a bright, glaring shine. His pants were pressed and the crease along their middle was sharp and straight. His shirt was new and had also been ironed, and he had rolled his sleeves evenly along both arms. A number of pins and badges decorated his uniform, and on his shoulders he bore the insignia of an inspector.

"Adam Lapid," he said, "I was told I might find you here. I'm Inspector Rosen, Tel Aviv Police. We need to have a word."

I had guessed who he was—there weren't that many police inspectors around who would have an interest in speaking with me—and I wondered how he'd learned I'd been sniffing around the Maryam Jamalka case. Was it the fat hotel manager, or had someone learned of my Holon meeting with Yossi Talmon? For now, it was best to feign ignorance of who Rosen was. I kept my face blank and took a slow sip of my coffee. Then I said, "What about?"

"I understand you've been asking questions about a certain young woman who was found dead a month ago in Tel Aviv," he said.

I nodded. "Maryam Jamalka."

His eyebrows twitched. He had expected me to deny conducting an investigation, not come right out and admit it.

"What's your interest in her?" he asked.

"I was hired to look into her murder."

"Hired by whom?"

"I'd rather not say."

He narrowed his eyes. "I'd rather you did. I might insist on it."

"Is that an official insistence?" I asked.

His eyes flashed in annoyance. "Whoever hired you to look into things is not important. I want you to stop investigating this case."

"Why?"

"I don't need to give you a reason. This is an open case, a police matter. Interfering with police work may lead to prosecution."

"I doubt I could interfere with anything. It's been over a month since the body was discovered, and, as I understand it, you guys don't even have a suspect in mind."

"Who told you that?" he demanded.

"Word gets around."

"Was it Yossi Talmon? Did he tell you that? He's in serious trouble if he did."

"Talmon?" I shook my head and snorted. "The man wouldn't even speak to me."

"Or maybe it was Reuben Tzanani. I understand you guys are close."

I could deny it, but I thought that would be a mistake. Rosen knew of my relationship with Reuben. He would never believe I hadn't asked Reuben for help with the case.

"I asked Reuben if he could connect me to the detective in charge of the investigation," I said. "He talked to Talmon, who refused to talk to me."

Rosen eyed me, trying to catch me at a lie. Policemen became quite adept at recognizing the telltale signs of liars. But I also knew those signs and kept my face clear of them.

"I don't need anyone in the investigation to tell me it's going nowhere," I said. "It's been a month. Most murders get solved within a few days or not at all. There have been no arrests so far, so I can assume that you guys have no suspects."

He didn't bother denying it. He was smarter than that. He took a breath, steadied himself, and tried another approach.

"Adam," he said, "may I call you Adam?"

I shrugged.

He said, "I've been told you were a policeman, Adam. In Europe somewhere."

I shrugged again.

"So you know that police work is not done in a vacuum. There are many factors to consider besides the crime itself."

"I don't follow you," I said.

"The police don't just solve crimes, they serve the public and its interests at large."

"Still not following you."

He crossed his arms. My eyes scrutinized his forearms. No number. "This case is a delicate one," he said. "The victim is the daughter of an important man, an Arab who has become a friend to Israel. I know you fought in the war. Got wounded even. Some say you were a hero."

There was a mocking edge to the way he pronounced the word *hero*, as if he was doubting I really could have been one or that, in his opinion, the respect given to heroes was exaggerated.

"I did my duty," I said.

His hands uncrossed and he pointed at me like a cartoon in a recruiting poster. "Well, now it's time for you to do your duty again."

The look he was giving me was so earnest, I almost burst out laughing. I had met Rosen's kind before, the mid-level officer— police or army, it didn't matter—who believed the rank he held bestowed upon him the ability to motivate men to do his bidding.

I quenched my smile and said, "The war is over, and I'm not a soldier anymore. And you're not an army officer."

His lips pressed together. "You have a duty as a citizen, and I am a police officer. A good citizen will do what I say."

"A good police officer would find and arrest Maryam Jamalka's killer."

"Don't tell me how to do my job. We know what we're doing."

"We?"

He nodded curtly. "We. This comes from high up."

"From whom?"

He waved a hand. "I cannot say. All you need to know is that it is the wish of people high up, very high up, that this matter is handled with discretion and care. So do what I say. Stay off this case. Stop asking questions about Maryam Jamalka. Leave this thing to us."

"I understand," I said.

"I don't need you to understand. I need you to obey."

"I'll think about it."

He sat back, staring at me. Color had crept into his cheeks. They were a ruddy hue now. One of his hands was on the table-top, and his fingers were half-curled into a fist. He looked about to burst.

But he didn't lose control. Instead he looked off to the side, and his fingers began drumming on the table. When he turned to look at me again, his eyes were hard flints, and his chin was tilted belligerently toward me.

"Don't play games with me, you imbecile," he said. "Who do you think you are? You think you're untouchable? You think taking a bullet or two in the War of Independence will protect you? You think you're still a hero? As you say, the war is over, and you're no longer a soldier. You're not even a policeman. You're just a civilian. If you keep interfering in this case, I will come down on you hard."

"What happened to all your talk about duty? I thought we were on the same side."

"You think this is funny? Keep this up and you might end up arrested."

"For what? Interfering with police business?" I shook my head. "That will make this case public, which is something you don't want. The people high up will blame you for it."

He put both elbows on the table and leaned forward so his head was halfway across the table to me. He smelled of cologne, and when he opened his mouth, I caught the scent of coffee and milk on his breath, commingled with some other familiar scent that I couldn't place, something rich and deep.

"You think I can't find something on you? Maybe you buy meat or coffee on the black market. Maybe you don't report all of your income. Maybe you keep a stash of illicit material under your bed. Don't push me. I can find something on anybody. Even when there is nothing to find."

I had met his kind of policeman before. They were the sort who saw no problem with planting evidence, writing false reports, employing deceitful witnesses, using force in their interrogation of suspects. They existed on every police force in every country. And the problem was that they knew how to work the system. They knew how to talk in court, how to present their evidence in a way that was hard to refute. They hid behind their immaculate uniform and badge and misused their power. And judges tended to believe every word that came out of their dirty, corrupted mouths.

He leaned back, smiling in satisfaction. "And just to be on the safe side, I will wreck the career of your friend Reuben Tzanani. I don't care whether he managed to convince Talmon to leak the case material to you or not. The mere fact that he went to talk to Talmon about an open case is bad enough in my book. He's a Yemenite, right? They always have lots of children. I wonder how he'll be able to care for them when he's out of work? And it will be your fault, Adam. All your fault. Just because you're a stubborn son of a bitch who can't leave well enough alone, can't follow simple instructions from those who know best."

He pushed his chair back and got to his feet. He looked down at me, and now there was just contempt in his eyes.

"She's not worth it, Adam. She was just a cheap whore. Nothing more. Sold her body to whatever stranger would pay her fee. What do you care what happened to her? It's foolish to ruin your life and the career of Reuben Tzanani for her."

"She deserves justice," I said.

He shrugged. "She's dead. She's beyond justice. Now you can either back off and spare yourself and others a whole pile of misery, or you can be stupid and go on an idiotic quest for some moronic young woman who got killed for being a whore."

He put his hands in his pockets, took a deep, chest-puffing breath, looked around him and said, "You like this café? You come here often?"

"Just about every day," I said.

He grinned and looked over his shoulder at where Greta was sitting near the door.

"I wonder if she gets some of her food on the black market. Maybe I should have a few inspectors look into it, what do you say?"

I said nothing. There was nothing to say. Rosen was prepared to use all his power and authority to get me to stop my investigation. And he had no qualms about hurting the people in my life to get his way.

He made a show of checking his watch. Its face was framed in silver and looked expensive. He smiled at me without separating his lips.

"Look at the time. And so much work to do. This is how it is with us real policemen. Busy, busy, busy. I'll leave you to your coffee. Enjoy the rest of your day."

He turned on his heel and strode out of the café. The bastard even made sure to smile at Greta and tell her how lovely the place looked before he stepped out into the street.

I watched him go, fuming. My mind was racing, trying to figure out what to do. I had not expected my investigation to remain secret forever, but I also did not anticipate the breadth of the threats made against me and people I cared about. Placing myself at risk was one thing. Risking others was quite another.

Greta came over to the table. "What was all that about? What did that officer want from you?"

"It's about the case with the Arab," I said. "He wants me to stop working on it."

"Why?"

"You don't want to know."

"Is it a security matter? Is the Arab some sort of terrorist?"

I snorted. "No. Nothing of the kind. Truly, Greta, you're better off not knowing the details."

She looked doubtful and perhaps a bit hurt, so I said, "If you knew, you might get into trouble."

"Trouble? With whom? The Arab?"

"Never mind." I grinned at her. "You can't leave well enough alone, can you? You need to know everything."

"Maybe I should have been a detective, like you."

"Maybe. But then who'd run the best café in Tel Aviv?"

The smile slowly faded from my lips when I recalled Rosen's threat to take action against Greta and her business.

"Tell me, Greta, do you use any black market products in the café?"

She looked at me. "Why do you ask?"

When a moment passed without me answering, she said, "I guess I could tell you it's none of your business, but the very words would feel foreign on my lips. Of course I use the black market. Doesn't everybody? Don't you?"

I nodded.

"Where did your question come from? What does this have to do with the police officer who just left here?"

"Why do you think it has anything to do with him?"

She gave me a pitying look and said, "Adam, if you're trying to hide something from me, it's better to just lie about it instead of evading the issue by answering my question with one of your own. Now you've got me worried. What have you gotten yourself into?"

I mulled over possible answers and discarded them one by one. Greta would not be fooled, and I wouldn't want to lie to her anyway. Leaving out my meeting with Talmon, I told her a little about the case and what Rosen threatened to do to her and the café if I didn't let it go. When I was done, Greta crossed her massive arms under her big breasts, and her lower lip pushed out as she thought over what I had just said.

Finally she said, "How close are you to solving this case?"

"I'm not sure," I said. "There is a chance I never will find out who killed her."

"But you've made progress?"

"I know more than I did when I started. And I had planned on learning even more tonight."

"Planned until this policeman came here with his threats?"

"Yes."

"And now you're rethinking things?"

"I don't want to see other people get hurt because of me."

"And if you don't proceed?" she asked.

"Then no one will ever find out who killed that girl."

"And other young women may die."

"Perhaps."

She tapped her forefinger against her lips, rubbing her arms as if she were cold. "I'm thinking about making some changes to the menu of the café," she said at length.

I frowned. "What changes?"

She smiled at me. Her crow's feet and the lines at the corners of her mouth deepened with her smile, and her eyes glinted with defiance. "Cutting some of the dishes off the menu. Temporarily."

I was beginning to understand and could feel a smile tugging at my lips. "And which dishes are you planning to cut?" I asked.

"Oh, I'll need to make a list. The cuts will be extensive, I fear. Anything that requires me to go to unsavory characters and acquire food items in a way which some may consider illegal."

"You'll be left with an abbreviated menu," I said.

She nodded gravely. "I think you're right. Still, it is a sacrifice I feel I must make. Rationing is unpleasant, but we're a new, poor country and if everyone just went off to the black market whenever they felt like it, what would our society be like?"

"Some would say it will be just fine, exactly like it is now."

"Perhaps. But my conscience would not let me rest if I went against the rules our benevolent government has set."

"I applaud your patriotism," I said, smiling. "Our country could use more people like you."

She glanced toward the door again, and when her face turned once more to me, no mirth remained in her eyes. "Our country has no use for people who kill young women. I'll take the risk of being badgered by the police. You just work quickly and try to bring this case to a swift end."

I opened my mouth to say I could make no promises, but she cut me off with her hand.

"I know, I know. There are no guarantees. No worthwhile venture is ever preordained for success. I had no idea this café would succeed when I started it, and we Jews had no assurance that we would have a country of our own when we set out to build it. Just do your best and as quickly as you can."

"It might not matter," I said. "Even if I find out who killed Maryam Jamalka, Rosen might still take it out on me, on you, and on Reuben. I know his kind. He's a vengeful sort. He would feel compelled to get back at me. And he will do it, partly, through you."

She let out a long breath. "I'll cross that bridge when I get to it," she said. "And if there is no bridge, I'll just have to swim across the river. The worst that will happen is I'll get a little wet."

Unless there are crocodiles in the river, I thought, but didn't say it. Greta was no fool. She was taking this risk with open eyes. I had never respected her as much as I did at that moment.

"All right. I'll do my best. Thank you, Greta."

She nodded twice, as if everything was settled. Then she said, "I wonder how the regulars will react to the new menu."

I couldn't help but smile. "There will be some grumbles."

"Nothing worse than grumbles?" she asked. "No one will choose to take his business elsewhere?"

"Not as many as one might suppose," I said, thinking that most of the regulars came to Greta's Café more for what Greta brought to it than for what was on the menu.

"I hope you're right," she said, and right then one of the regulars, a man named Yoel, entered the café and called his hello to Greta and me. She rose and said, "It's good that Yoel is here. He eats a lot. He'll help me get through my supplies faster." She went to tend to Yoel, and I closed the chessboard, put it in its box, and stashed the box behind the bar where Greta kept it for me. Then I went out in search of a telephone.

This time Reuben picked up.

"It's about time you got back to me," he said. "What took you so long? We need to talk. There's trouble."

"Let me guess," I said. "You had a chat with Inspector Rosen."

"More like he had a chat with me," he said, lowering his voice. "A rather unpleasant chat, I must say."

"Can you talk?"

"I think so. Give me a second to close the door." When he came back, he said, "How did you know about Rosen? He talked to you?"

"About thirty minutes ago. At Greta's." I described my conversation with Rosen and related the threats he'd made against Reuben.

"You gave him a similar story to the one I did," Reuben said when I was done. "At least that's something."

"Not that it matters to him. It won't stop him from carrying out his threats."

"No. I suppose it won't."

I didn't tell him about the go-ahead I got from Greta. I didn't want him to feel pressured to place his career at risk for me and my case.

He said, "You know, Adam, I've met all sorts of police officers during my time on the force, but I have never met someone like him. The way he came in here and questioned me, it was like I were a criminal and he wanted to put me away in jail."

"I'm sorry you had to go through this, Reuben," I said, recalling the conversation I'd had with him before meeting Yossi Talmon. Reuben had told me then he did not want to be caught in the middle of some interdepartmental mess. Now he was, and I felt responsible.

"It's not your fault. Rosen didn't learn of my talk with Talmon from you. He already guessed that you came to me for help. I guess too many people have seen me with you. Maybe I should start avoiding you."

"It may do wonders for your career," I said.

He sighed wearily, and I could hear the strain in his voice. Rosen had put genuine fear into him. And that made me feel like tearing the inspector's insignia off his shoulders and forcing him to eat it. Reuben had more to worry about than Greta did. Greta's children were grown and leading their own lives. Reuben was the breadwinner of his family, the provider of four young children. And because he was a policeman, and only a corporal at that, his livelihood was in clear jeopardy if he dared go against Inspector Rosen's wishes.

"I just don't understand it," he said. "Since when do petty politics come before finding a murderer?"

"In Hungary the police used to make allowances for politicians and rich men all the time," I said.

"For murder?"

"I don't know of any such case, but it may have happened."

"Did you ever do that, Adam? When you were a policeman?"

"No," I said. "Never for murder. And never for political reasons. But I did turn a blind eye on smaller things. Looking back, it's not something I'm proud of, Reuben, but it's the truth. Sometimes I did it for information and sometimes for other things. But I never closed my eyes on murder. That is unthinkable."

He digested this for a moment. When he spoke, his tone had an accusatory edge to it, as if he were disappointed in me. "Well, I never did any of those things, and I certainly did not join the police department to disregard murder." He paused for a beat. "So tell me if I can help you any further in your investigation."

My grin was wide enough to feel it in my cheeks. "You do like to stick your neck out for me, don't you, Reuben?"

He let out a nervous little laugh. "So it seems. But compared to that other time, this one doesn't look all that scary."

In that other time bullets and artillery shells were flying everywhere around us, men were getting killed and maimed, and

Reuben was carrying my bleeding, inert self on his back to find someone to plug the two holes in me.

"I owe you one for this, Reuben."

"I'll add it to your favors tab."

"Do that. As for helping me with the investigation, I need you to take a look at Maryam Jamalka's arrest." I told him about the arrest that took place at Club Adom, how Akiva and Lydia said it had been unusual, and gave him the dates of the arrest and Maryam's release from jail.

"What am I looking for?" Reuben asked.

"I don't know. But something happened during that time that changed her life. I need to know what it was. If I come up with a specific question, I'll let you know."

"Okay. I'll start sniffing around. But I'll need to do it carefully. If Rosen catches wind of it..."

Then Reuben would be suspended, if not fired, and wouldn't be able to help me any further.

"Then be careful. One more thing: get in touch with Talmon and tell him that as long as he sticks to what I told Rosen, he's in the clear."

"You hope," Reuben said.

"I hope. It's the best I can do."

"You can do better. You can catch this guy."

"I'll do my best, Reuben."

I ended the call and made my way home, feeling buoyed. Rosen had thought he could make me back off by issuing threats against me, Greta, and Reuben. But it appeared that the people closest to me were not the sort to bend or buckle easily. Neither was I. Apparently Rosen did not know or appreciate my history. I had been through much worse than anything he could throw at me. His threats did not move or scare me. And now that I knew I had the go-ahead from both Greta and Reuben, I felt unstoppable. I was going to catch this killer, and if I ruffled Inspector

Rosen's feathers, or those of his superiors, in the process, so be it.

I got home around four and sat at my table with my Western. It was a short book, and I got through it by six. In the end the good guy shot the bad man down and rode off in search of other adventures. That was how many of these books ended—some sort of showdown between good and evil, with good prevailing. It was unrealistic, and I often wondered why I liked reading these stories. Maybe I was hoping life could become that way. Because it sure wasn't that way now.

At nine o'clock I went out to find Charlie Buzaglo. And I had my knife and gun with me.

# 16

I didn't expect him to be there. I thought I'd have to visit a whole batch of nightclubs in Jaffa in order to find him. But Charlie Buzaglo was sitting at the same club where I'd last met him, the one I went to first just to eliminate it from the mental list of places that I had prepared.

He was seated alongside the same pretty young woman he had been with then. He was wearing a cream-colored shirt and had the top three buttons open. She had on a black dress that rode halfway up her crossed legs. He had a hand on her thigh. She had both hands on the tabletop. I went straight to his table and planted myself in a chair.

"Tell her to give us some privacy," I said.

He squinted his eyes at me, lifted his drink, and took a slow, measured sip. "We're in the middle of a conversation, and you're not wanted here."

"We are going to talk about Maryam Jamalka. Remember her? One of your prostitutes. Well, she's dead." I turned to the girl. "Do you want to end up dead, too? Because that's what happens to women who hang around Charlie too long."

Her doe eyes got even wider, and she started to ask Buzaglo something, but he raised a hand to quiet her. She paused for a beat, then started talking again. He turned his rat eyes on her and said, "I told you to shut your mouth, so keep it shut. Now go to the bar. Get a drink. And don't talk to anyone else this time. Got it?"

Her eyes sparkled wetly and her lower lip trembled, but she kept silent. She grabbed her purse and left the table. She didn't go to the bar but headed straight to the bathroom, where no one could see her cry, and where she could redo her face.

Buzaglo wasn't smiling this time as he watched her leave. And he wasn't smiling when he turned his eyes back to me.

"Two broken ribs," he said.

"You were lucky. I could have broken all of them and busted your knees as well. How is your friend, by the way?"

"The useless moron has a limp, but he'll be all right. He's lucky I was in a charitable mood, or he wouldn't be walking around at all. And neither would you, Adam. You must be the stupidest man in Israel to come here again. Or did you think that you could ambush me a second time?"

"If you want to go outside and face me one on one, like honorable men do, I won't need to."

"I like it here just fine," Buzaglo said. "Or at least I did before you showed up."

"Answer some questions and I'll be on my way."

"About Maryam?"

"Yes. About Maryam."

He seemed to mull it over, and I expected him to refuse to answer any of my questions. But he surprised me by saying, "Maryam. Now that was a sweet girl. Very popular with men. Made good money for me, she did. It's too bad that she's dead."

His mouth had dropped open a bit, and his eyes appeared to

protrude from their sockets more than they usually did. He looked more like a rat than ever before.

"You don't seem surprised by her death."

He shrugged. "It makes sense."

"What does that mean?" I asked.

"I haven't seen her for weeks. I figured something might have happened."

"She could have run out on you."

"No one runs out on me."

"Except Mordecai Ohayon," I said, referencing the man Buzaglo had wanted me to give into his hands, the one I allowed to escape.

"You will pay dearly for that, Adam. And for my ribs."

I ignored his threat. "You also don't seem surprised to see me here."

"No. I thought you might show up."

"The hotel manager. The Jaffa Star. He told you I was asking around."

He wagged a finger at me. "You should stop hurting people, Adam. It makes them hate you. He says you nearly broke his fingers. He also swore he didn't mention my name. But I figured you'd find me all the same. Who gave you my name?"

"An upstanding citizen," I said. "How did you become Maryam's pimp?"

"I first had her as a customer. She was beautiful. Lovely skin and great eyes. Good body." His eyes turned toward the bar, where the young woman now sat with a drink, eyes downcast. "Revital is also beautiful, but not like Maryam, and not as easy to manipulate. Maryam was easy. The moment I saw her, I could sense how vulnerable she was. Some of them are like that. They want to be loved. All she needed to hear was that I loved her, and she would do anything for me."

"Why did you move her out of her apartment?"

"In order to control her. That apartment was part of her life before she met me. I wanted her to be close to me, in a place where I could control her fully. I moved her to an apartment house in Jaffa. Not nice like her previous apartment. Just one room and the neighbors can get noisy, but she didn't complain. I got the impression she'd lived in worse places in her life."

I gazed at the girl at the bar. She was now watching the band play. Was she also hungry enough for love to be manipulated and controlled by a low-life like Charlie Buzaglo? My stomach felt queasy. If I had known Charlie Buzaglo was a pimp, I never would have done a job for him.

I looked at him. He was looking right back at me, his face placid, but there was just a hint of a smile on his thin lips. He was enjoying this; he found it amusing to answer my questions. I had expected this to be more of a struggle, perhaps with him denying even knowing anyone named Maryam Jamalka, and me using the knowledge I'd gotten so far to squeeze the answers from him. But he was answering me freely and openly. And I didn't know why.

"Give me the address where she lived," I said.

"No. But it wouldn't help you if I did. She hasn't been there in weeks. And none of her stuff is there any longer."

"Since she was arrested?"

"Yes," he said after a brief hesitation. "Since then."

"What happened when she was arrested?"

"What do you mean?"

"The arrest was unusual. Most arrested prostitutes don't spend time in jail. She was locked up for three days."

He shrugged. "This time it was different. Who can say why?"

"She was different when she got out, and you were no longer seen with her. Why? What happened?"

He shrugged again, but this time his lips compressed. I had touched upon a sore point.

"Did she no longer want to be with you?" I said.

"You don't know what you're talking about."

"Did she tell you to stay away from her? Did she finally see you for the rat that you are?"

He sat straight in his chair and pointed a finger at me. "You're a fool. She begged me to take her back. Begged me. Wept and pleaded. I wouldn't have taken her back even if—"

He stopped in mid-sentence, his face sour, like a man angry, not at someone else, but at himself.

"Even if what?"

He sat back, glancing away. "I'm done talking to you."

"No," I said. "You're not done. I want to know why you wouldn't take her back. She could still make money for you. You wouldn't give her up for no reason."

"Enough with your questions. I said we're done talking."

I leaned forward. "You don't seem to get it, Charlie. I am going to find out what happened to her. And you're going to help me. Do you understand? Or are two broken ribs not enough motivation for you?"

He gritted his teeth, and his eyes shone with rage. "Just because you got lucky once, doesn't mean that you would get lucky again. I won't be following you into a dark alley this time. I'm staying right here in this club, where there are plenty of men who would gladly lend a hand to bash you if you make any trouble for me."

"You're going to sit in this club forever?" I asked. "Because I will get the information from you."

"Not forever. But you won't be around to watch me leave. Soon I will have someone throw you out. So leave now, on your own two feet, or be thrown out on your ass."

I looked around me. There were about a dozen young men in the place, and I figured at least half would gang up on me if Buzaglo and I started fighting. For the moment I was beaten. And I could tell by his face that he knew that I knew it. He smiled an indulgent, self-satisfied smile at me. It made me furious, itching to reach over the table and slap that smile off his face along with some of his teeth. But I wouldn't get any information that way. I had to retreat, temporarily.

I pushed my chair back and rose.

He said, "You were a fool to come here, Adam. But I'm glad that you did. I'm very glad that you did."

He was grinning at me now, showing his uneven teeth. I wanted to tell him that we weren't finished, partly to get the last word in. But I refrained. Saying the words would not help me. I was on his turf, and he had the advantage. I would have to get him in another location at a later time and question him again.

Outside the club, I paused on the sidewalk to light a cigarette. I walked slowly, keeping my ears open, waiting to hear the sound of the nightclub door open and close, signifying that someone had come out after me. This time, though, there was nothing, just the hum and buzz of the city around me and the thud of my shoes on the dirty, dust-clogged pavement.

I hastened my steps, heading north, sucking on the cigarette so hard that its taste disgusted me. I tossed it only half spent, and it bounced on the road, flashing out its little burst of sparks before dying out.

My mind went over my conversation with Charlie Buzaglo. He had given me little. In fact, it seemed to me that the only reason he spoke with me at all was to flaunt his domination over Maryam Jamalka, to gloat over it. He knew it would infuriate me. He wanted to get under my skin. It was his revenge for those two broken ribs. Or part of his revenge, as he had said I would pay for those ribs at some later time.

The bad taste stayed in my mouth long after I had discarded the cigarette. It was an aftertaste of my encounter with Buzaglo. Just the thought of him taking advantage of Maryam Jamalka sickened me. He might not have killed her, but his exploitation of her had contributed to her death. This I knew in my gut. It was a certainty of emotion rather than one of fact. As Sima Vaaknin had told me, he had used Maryam Jamalka's romanticism to gain control over her life.

Sima Vaaknin.

The thought of her brought me to a stop. I was five minutes away from my apartment and the fitful sleep that awaited me in my empty bed. My watch told me it was after eleven. Too late to pay an unannounced visit on anyone, but perhaps, like the night on which Akiva had telephoned her on my behalf, Sima Vaaknin would not be asleep.

But I didn't want to see Sima Vaaknin. She was dangerous. Hard to resist. Perhaps even addictive. If I went to her, it would be for one purpose only. And there would be guilt afterward. Scorching, searing guilt. The kind that would infiltrate my dreams and make me wish I could tear all memories of my wife out of me and erase my past and the love I had lost. I wanted to avoid this guilt and decided to go home. But my legs took me past the turn to Hamaccabi Street and further north, through nearly deserted late night streets, all the way to her building.

On the sidewalk outside, I paused and raised my eyes. Her windows were dark. Was she asleep, or had she company? Either choice likely meant that I would be unwelcome. I went up the stairs and knocked on her door.

A minute or so went by with no answer. I felt a flash of disappointment that was supplanted by a rush of relief. I was halfway down the stairs when I heard her voice at my back.

# 17

"Running away, Adam?"

I didn't know how she had recognized me from the back. I turned and she was in the doorway, her hair mussed and beautifully chaotic, the contours of a pillow's edge marking a soft indentation on her cheek. She was wearing a blue nightshirt that left her legs bare to mid-thigh. My eyes lingered on her legs, consuming the lines of her feet and calves, the graceful knobs of her knees, before traveling up to her covered hips and to where her breasts hung free and firm beneath her shirt. When my eyes reached her face, her full-lipped mouth was split into the satisfied smile of the appreciated, and the deep brown pools of her eyes shone with amusement. She had caught my admiring appraisal of her, and she relished it.

Before opening her door, she had turned on the light inside her apartment. Its light far outmatched that of the weak staircase bulb, and her shadow was thrown across the landing and stairs, brushing my shoes with its hazy darkness.

"You should not open the door to strangers, dressed like

that," I said, my mouth so dry I was surprised my voice did not crack.

"But I knew it was you."

"How?"

She tapped the peephole with her forefinger. "With this."

I felt heat rush to my face. So she hadn't recognized me from the back after all.

"Then why did it take you so long to open the door?"

She smiled, and the fingers of her left hand brushed the fabric of her nightshirt over the valley made by her breasts. "I had to put this on first."

The heat from my face went south to my belly and further down past my belt buckle.

"And now you'd better come in. You rousted me out of bed, and I'd like to return to it before too long."

She pulled the door further open, holding it for me, letting me consider whether she meant to return to bed by herself or with me for company.

When I passed by her on the threshold, I caught her scent—soap, and not the cheap, utilitarian one given each citizen as part of their rations, and the clean, wholesome smell of freshly laundered sheets. She did not look like a woman whose sleep had been disturbed. Her eyes were alert, and the skin of her face showed none of the slackness of the recently awakened.

I wondered how I smelled, how I looked. Had the smells of the nightclub in which I had met Charlie Buzaglo clung to me? Was I sweaty after my long walk to Sima's apartment? And how did my fitful sleep and stressful days mark my face?

If there was anything, Sima showed no sign of being repelled by it. She gestured for me to sit on the sofa, telling me she would make me some tea.

I nodded and she returned a moment later with two mugs. She

had added cold water to each cup, so the tea was pleasantly warm instead of scorching, and we could drink without waiting for it to cool. She had liberally sweetened the tea with honey. It was almost too sweet, like candy, but I drank it down hungrily just the same. She sipped her own delicately, scrutinizing me over the lip of her mug.

She was sitting next to me on the sofa, close enough I could feel the warmth of her body radiating off her skin. The line of the pillow had faded from her cheek, and her skin was now an unblemished dark shade, like melted chocolate.

"I expected you last night," she said.

"I never said I would come."

"But I invited you."

This she said as a simple statement of fact, a sufficient basis on which to assume that I would come. Her tone was tinged with bewilderment. She was not used to men resisting her, not even for a single night.

"I did not intend to come here tonight, either," I said.

"No. I can see that you're not sure you should be here. You sit like a man who thinks he should be on his feet. But you don't want to leave, do you?"

I said nothing, and that was answer enough.

"You didn't come here tonight for me," she said, peering at my face. "At least not just for me. Something happened tonight. Something that left a taste of anger and frustration in your mouth."

I glanced at her sharply. "How can you tell all that?"

She shrugged, and her breasts shifted the cloth of the night-shirt. "It is not hard to see. You wear your feelings on your face, as you do your history on your arm."

I was wearing a jacket now, but I hadn't been when I came to this apartment the first time. I looked into her eyes, checking to see if there was pity or scorn there. I had gotten such looks before from those Jews who had been lucky enough not to know the camps, who were used to fighting as equals, to returning blow for blow, to being victorious. Sima's eyes showed none of that. If there was anything but curiosity, and a touch of anticipation, I could not detect it.

"I had a chat with Maryam's pimp."

She drew a sharp breath. "Just now?"

"Just now. It turns out I knew him from before."

I explained a little bit about my history with Charlie Buzaglo, how he had tried to attack me, and the broken ribs he wound up with as a result.

Sima laughed when I told her of the broken ribs. "Oh, good. He deserved it." She turned serious. "And Maryam?"

"I don't know yet. There is something I'm missing. Some connection that I'm failing to make. And there is something that Buzaglo knows but wouldn't tell me."

"So how will you know?"

"I'll get the information. Don't worry about that," I told her flatly, and she arched an eyebrow but didn't ask for clarification.

She sipped her tea and I did the same with mine.

I looked at her and asked myself whether she was feeling any remorse about severing her relationship with Maryam when she got involved with Buzaglo. She shouldn't. Fighting for Maryam would have been a lost cause. And it would have brought Buzaglo into Sima's life. He would have tried to make her his servant. I didn't think he would have succeeded. Sima Vaaknin was not the hopeless romantic Maryam Jamalka had been, and could not be manipulated by her emotions. But he would have tried all the same.

This led me to wonder how Sima Vaaknin wound up a prostitute. I knew Maryam Jamalka's story and could not imagine Sima following a similar path. But I didn't ask, and if she read the question on my face, she showed no sign of it.

She finished her tea and set her mug on the coffee table. She plucked the mug from my hand. It was still a third full, but I didn't protest. She set it down next to hers and looked up at me.

"Come," she said simply, and extended her hand. I took it, and her fingers entwined themselves around mine. They were cool, but her palm was warm.

She led me down a hall toward a rear room.

It was dark within, but I could make out the outline of a large bed, the covers bunched on one side. The room smelled clean and fresh. If other men had been there earlier that night, their presence had been expunged. There was just me and Sima now.

"I want the lights on," she said, and flicked them on without waiting for my approval.

The room was simply furnished—a nightstand, a number of shelves bearing white candles in their saucers. A radio on a dresser. The bedsheets were white, the pillowcases red. The curtains were drawn and of a darker shade of red than the pillowcases. There were no pictures on the walls. No books. No ornaments. Sima was the only thing that drew the eye.

The light made me think of my scars. Would she be repelled by them? She did not allow me time to make up my mind. She pulled her nightshirt over her head, tossed it aside, and stood before me, naked and unembarrassed.

I took in her breasts, her stomach, the juncture of her thighs. She came to me, drew the jacket off my shoulders, and allowed it to slip to the floor. She grabbed the back of my head, fingers in my hair, and pulled my head down while rising on tiptoes.

The kiss was short and awkward. I was to blame. Her lips were soft and inviting, mine were unresponsive. She drew back and looked up at me.

"Now, let's try it again."

She kissed me again, pressing her body tightly into mine, and pried my lips apart with her tongue. She tasted of honey. My arms went around her, feeling the smooth texture of her back, the supple softness of her buttocks.

"That was better," she said, once we broke the kiss. "But you are still holding something back."

She did not sound accusatory, but challenged.

"Kick off your shoes," she said, and I complied, following the shoes with my pants and socks and shorts.

She smiled, pleased at my obvious desire. She unbuttoned my shirt and pulled it off me. Now I was as naked as she. She ran her eyes over me, lingering on the scars on my torso, but didn't say anything.

She took me by the hand and pushed me onto the bed. She came on top of me and kissed me, running her hands over me. My body responded with a hunger of its own, but I kept a part of me distant, not allowing myself to fully drown in the moment.

She ceased her kisses and pulled back to a sitting position, straddling me. She examined my face, arching an eyebrow.

"You're not married," she said, and for once she sounded unsure of herself.

She was right, both in her words and in her self-doubt. I was not married. My wife, Deborah, had been dead for five years, likely on the very day in which the train that took us from Hungary came to its final stop in Auschwitz. Common sense and social proprieties dictated that five years was long enough for mourning. But apparently, it was not long enough for me.

As I kissed Sima Vaaknin and felt her body with my hands, the face of my Deborah flashed through my mind. I knew she wouldn't blame me for permitting myself the promise of pleasure this night held, but I could blame myself well enough. I wanted to feed the hunger of my body, but not to allow myself to feast on Sima Vaaknin. And I wanted to feast on her, to taste every part of her, to touch her and smell her and sense her every way I could. But doing so would mean crossing a line I wanted to keep from crossing. It would mean I was putting Deborah more firmly in the past, that I was relegating her and our love to a thing that was rather than a thing that is. So I was about to take a measure of delight and no more, enough to quench a thirst without getting drunk.

But Sima had other plans. As I kissed her again, slowly and cautiously, letting myself go only so far, she broke off our kiss, raised her head above mine, and said to me, "This won't do, Adam. It won't do at all," and proceeded to break down my resistance with her hands and mouth and in-depth knowledge of the male anatomy.

My resolve to keep a part of me from her turned brittle and crumbled. I quickly lost track of time and everything else apart from Sima. Later, I realized that I had offended her professionally, both by taking two nights instead of one to accept her invitation, and by my attempt to give her just a part of myself. In her bed, she was the one who determined how far things went, how much pleasure to give, and how much to receive. Her clients thought they were in control, but what they bought was the right to be controlled by her. She knew exactly how much of herself to give to each one, how much they really wanted to accept. She never gave all she had. But she was the only one allowed to do so. I had lost that right when I stepped over her threshold.

For the next hour or so, I was adrift in Sima. When we finally broke off, gasping and sweaty, I lay on my back, staring at her ceiling, listening to my breaths and the pounding rhythm of my heart upon my eardrums. A part of me felt like weeping, another wanted to ask Deborah for forgiveness. A third part made me turn to Sima, who lay beside me with a smile of victory and conquest on her lips, and say, "Let's do it again."

# 18

Afterward Sima Vaaknin asked, "How did you get those?" She was sitting in bed, devoid of any modesty, her naked breasts glistening with sweat, her supple legs elastically curled close to her body. She was pointing at my torso. At my two scars.

"In the war," I said.

She reached over and ran her fingers over the pink, ridged, warped skin. Her expression was one of utter fascination. She licked her lips, and the tip of her skillful tongue protruded out of her mouth like a turtle's head.

"What are they from? Tell me how you got them."

"Both are bullet wounds," I said. "I got them on the same day, when we were fighting the Egyptian Army in the south."

"They don't look like they were caused by the same thing. This one is much bigger."

She was touching the scar that ran a little below my belly button. It was a horizontal line, five inches in length. The other scar, the one on my chest, was the shape and size of a flattened coin. The stomach scar looked the worse of the two, but looks were like human beings—they could be deceiving. My chest wound was the one that had nearly ended my life, that put me in the hospital in critical condition for a week and kept me there for another month. The stomach wound was minor in comparison.

"Here," I said, pointing to my stomach, "the bullet went in from the side, ran through the skin and tissue beneath, and came out the other end. Here," I pointed at my chest, "it got me straight, almost like I'd been stabbed with the point of a dagger. That's why it went in deeper and did more damage."

I studied her face as she looked at my scars. There was not a trace of disgust or dismay in her eyes. She seemed mesmerized, awed. As if she were looking at a work of art or a natural phenomenon that arrested the eye and excited the mind. Which was what she was, with her unblemished, smooth skin, her taut feline limbs, her large fathomless eyes—a natural phenomenon, a work of art.

"Did it hurt very much?" she asked.

I frowned. It was a strange question, as the answer seemed obvious. I got the sense that Sima did not ask me for a confirmation of what she'd already guessed, but because she derived some pleasure from hearing me utter the words. She was used to seeing men exposed, and this was just another form of nakedness.

"Not at first. The heat of battle muffled the pain, and then I was out, bleeding on the ground, half dead and half alive. Later, in the hospital, it hurt. Very much."

I didn't add that right at that moment, perhaps due to her questions or her attention, both scars ached.

She caressed the scars some more, feeling their contours with as much attention and skill as her hands had displayed across other parts of my anatomy shortly before. Was she studying them like a blind man would study a face for later recognition?

"And this?" she asked, brushing a plum-colored bruise on my breastbone with her fingers. "This is new."

I explained how I had gotten the bruise fighting Maryam's pimp and one of his flunkies.

"That's when you broke his ribs?" she asked.

"Yes."

Sima pulled her hands back to her lap. She raised her eyes to mine. "Show me your back."

I stiffened. "What for?"

"I felt it when we were making love." Her black eyes were glinting like snake skin. "I want to see."

I didn't move. She pouted.

"Come on," she said. "It's not like I haven't seen everything else. And you aren't ashamed of those." She pointed at my battle scars. "Why can't I see the ones on your back? Do you think they're ugly?"

That wasn't it. I hardly ever looked at them, and not because they were uglier than the ones on my front, though uglier they were. How could I explain to Sima Vaaknin that scars were the perfect reminder? It was no accident that God chose to mark Cain's skin. It was not just so others would know of Cain's sin in killing Abel, his brother. It was also so Cain would be reminded of it whenever he saw his reflection in a pool of water, whenever he rubbed or scratched his forehead, whenever he saw the frown in the face of a new acquaintance. The scars on my chest and stomach reminded me of being a soldier, of fighting for independence, of having the ability to defend myself. The ones on my back reminded me of being powerless, fearful, at the mercy of devils in human skin, of being less than a man. But there was no point in hiding them from her. Her fingers had already memorized their shape and length and outline. Having her see them would do me no harm. I sat up, turned my back to her, and heard her sharp intake of breath as she saw my ravaged skin.

Her quick fingers darted over my back. At first, there was hesitation in her touch. She had shown none during our lovemaking. She was an expert at it, experienced beyond tentative-ness. But this was something new for her, and I could feel—what? A reverential wonderment in her touch?

"My God," she said breathlessly. "I have never seen anything like it."

Her fingers, emboldened now, scurried over the web of inter-lacing scars on my back, tracing each ridged line. They were put there by a sadistic Austrian camp guard. He had used a whip he'd always carried with him as he walked about the camp. I couldn't say how many lashes he had dealt me. The scars could not answer this question, as they crisscrossed each other in such a tight weave that it was difficult to tell where some began and others ended.

"How did you get these?" she said, her hands still roaming over my scars.

My skin crawled, and I turned and caught her wrists. "Enough."

She blinked, looking at me with her big eyes wider still.

"I'll trade you," she said. "One horrible story for another."

I frowned at her, puzzled.

"You want to know how I got to be what I am. I saw the look in your eyes earlier. You want to know but dare not ask the ques-tion. Your instinct was correct. I wouldn't have told you. But if you tell me how you got those scars on your back, I will tell you how my life turned out the way it has."

Her eyes were sparkling. She knew she had dangled a bait that I would be tempted to reach for. Like a feint in battle, the one the enemy falls for, leaving his flank exposed.

I nodded my head slowly, accepting her offer.

"I'll go first," she said, like a child rushing to secure her posi-tion on a swing, and began telling her story.

She spoke in a flat, emotionless tone, as if what she was telling did not happen to her but to some faraway stranger. Her story had the fuzzy edges of a tale oft repeated, whose form and substance changed as it passed from one set of lips to another set of ears over and over again. I felt certain Sima Vaaknin had not told this story to many people. But she might have told it to herself a great many times over the years and had embellished and refined it along the way. She did not falter once in seeking the perfect word to use. She was practiced in the telling of this story, and in the hearing of it, even if only inside her head.

Her story began in 1929, when Sima was seven years old. She and her family lived in the city of Hebron, in the Jewish neighborhood that had existed there for centuries, close to the Cave of Machpelah, where the Jewish biblical Patriarchs—Abraham, Isaac, and Jacob—and the Jewish Matriarchs—Sarah, Leah, and Rivkah—were said to be entombed. In August of that year, riots broke out throughout the country, as Arabs, inflamed by religious leaders, attacked Jews in Tel Aviv, Jerusalem, Safed, and a variety of small towns and villages. The Jewish communities of Jenin, Gaza, and Nablus had to be evacuated by the British to ensure their safety.

But Hebron saw the worst of the rioting. In that city, an Arab mob armed with knives, axes, and pitchforks stormed Jewish homes and institutions, murdering men, women, and children. Some were tortured, and many of the bodies were mutilated. Women and young girls were raped before they were killed. Some Jews were killed in close proximity to the local British police, who did little to defend them during the worst of the rioting.

Sima Vaaknin was the oldest daughter of her family. She had two small brothers and one sister. Sima's father was a baker. Arab rioters broke into his bakery and pushed him into his burning oven. Her mother was at home with Sima and her siblings. Arabs broke into their home, murdered her two brothers and sister before her mother's and Sima's eyes, then raped her mother and Sima. After the rape, an Arab armed with a steel club stove

Sima's mother's head in. Sima remembered him as a giant looming over her, his face craggy and massive, his features engorged and grotesque. In truth, I imagined, he was a regular-sized man made monstrously tall by a child's recollection, further distorted by trauma.

"I don't know why they did not kill me," Sima said in her distant tone, "but I managed to escape the house through a window. I ran without direction through the streets. They were full of crashing noises, cries of pain, pleading for help. And smoke. There was smoke everywhere. Whenever I heard angry shouts in Arabic, I clung to the walls and made myself small. I hurt so bad everywhere, inside and out. It was hard to move. After running for a long time, I was exhausted. I lay down next to a house, brought my legs to my chest, hugged myself, and waited, trembling, for things to calm."

She trembled a bit now, and a higher tone invaded her words, as if the child she'd been was talking to me from twenty years in the past.

"After a while," she went on, "a hand shook me. Told me to get up quickly. It was an Arab man, short, slim, with a thin mustache. I didn't want him to touch me. I didn't want him to hurt me. But I had no strength left. He picked me up, held me to his chest, and walked quickly away with me in his arms. He got to an old house, knocked on the door, and an Arab woman—his wife, I later learned—opened the door, and we went in and descended to the cellar. A number of frightened Jews huddled inside, sitting on the floor, while the wife made coffee and tea. His name was Abu Id Zaitoun, and I owe him and his family my life. Why they did it—why they risked their lives for us—I do not know. But they kept me and others safe until the British evacuated us to the police station. I never returned to Hebron again."

She paused, her eyes on some point on the wall behind me, or on the past behind the present.

I said nothing. I knew a little about the 1929 riots, but I had not heard any personal accounts. And I had not known the gory and gruesome details, the extent of the brutality. Now I understood what Sima had meant when she said that she'd taken Maryam Jamalka in because she had a debt to pay. The debt was to Abu Id Zaitoun and his family, and if they could not be repaid for saving her life, she would help another Arab in their place. I also understood what had happened to her sister.

But Sima's story wasn't done. She said, "After the riots ended, I was given to a Jewish family in Haifa. They had one girl called Carmella. She was eleven years old when I arrived. The father of the family used to visit our room at night and go to her bed. I would hear them from under the blanket I had pulled over my head. I lay there shivering until he was done with her. Then I heard her weep herself back to sleep. I told her mother about it, but she slapped my face, told me to stop telling lies, and threatened to kick me out on the street if I told anyone. I was ten when he switched from Carmella to me. Then I was truly alone, because she resented it. Carmella, I mean. She hated me more than she hated her father. As if I had taken him from her. I would have gladly given him up if I only could.

"I was thirteen when I ran away. I drifted from one place to another for a time. Stayed in a kibbutz, but left before long. I ended up in Tel Aviv and became what I am today. First I worked for a man who had a number of women and girls working for him. He was rough and scary but was only violent if a girl tried to leave. Otherwise he would be afraid of marking us with his blows. It would make us less desirable to men. But eventually I became free when he died in a fight with another criminal. And since then I have been working for myself. No one controlling me. Free."

She paused and a silence as deep as a well fell in the room. Then she blinked a few times, her face twitched, and her posture, rigid throughout her narration, softened. She turned her eyes to me and smiled expectantly. "Your turn."

I looked at her for a moment, speechless. I was stunned by the abrupt shift in her demeanor. I felt a mixture of horror and sadness and anger. But if Sima Vaaknin was feeling anything, I could not tell it from her face or body.

"Come on," she said after a moment. "You're not a cheater, are you? You promised to tell me your story if I told you mine."

I swallowed hard and nodded.

"Mine is not nearly as long as yours," I said. This was true only because I was not going to tell her the whole story. I was not going to talk about being stuffed into a train car with dozens of other Jews. I was not going to tell her how I had lost my family. I was not going to talk about all the horrors I had witnessed at the camp. It was not what I had agreed to, and it would take too long anyway.

"Just tell it," she said, and she lay down on her side, her hands tucked under her head, looking like a child eager to hear a bedtime story. I half expected her to yawn like children do, without covering her mouth.

I started to talk. I told Sima Vaaknin a little about the camp. I told her of being hungry and tired and depressed and hopeless. I told her of being reduced to an animal, a stinking, filthy, sick shell of a man. I told her about the guard—his brown shock of hair, his pocked skin, his blue eyes, his cruel mouth with the small, sharp teeth, the way he would slap his thigh with the whip, the vulgar insults he would hurl at prisoners.

"I saw him," I said, "saw him roam the camp, seeking any excuse to beat a prisoner. Some of the guards simply did what they were told. No more, no less. But he belonged to another group— those who relished the power they'd been given over us and enjoyed using it. Enjoyed inflicting pain on those of us whom they considered less than men. So I tried to steer clear of him. But one day he came up behind me, ordered me to remove my shirt and kneel down. If I did something to provoke him, I don't know what it was. He wasn't the sort who needed a reason, really. And there would be no one to discipline him if I died. My life was worthless. Why he chose to punish me with a whip and not a gun, I do not know. Maybe it was because he wanted me to suffer for long, and death is so final. Say what you will of death, at least it ends pain."

I paused and glanced at her. Her expression was hard to read, but it was clear that she did not understand the whole story. She did not understand what the camp was like. This was why I didn't like to talk about Auschwitz with those who hadn't been there. It was like talking to a creature from another planet. There was no basis for understanding.

But there was also no pity in her eyes, no sadness, only blank curiosity. There was a wall within Sima Vaaknin, I realized, a place behind which part of her emotions were safely stored away where they couldn't hurt. And those emotions were not brought out for anyone. Not for her, and not for me.

"And it hurt a lot?" she asked.

"Yes. It hurt a whole lot. Not just when the whip sliced into my skin, but for a long time after. It hurt worse than the bullet wounds."

She rose without a word and went to the bathroom. I heard the toilet flush and water running into the sink. She returned and sat by me on the bed. She looked me straight in the eye and laid a hand on my thigh. There was a question in her eyes. *Do you still want me?* she seemed to ask. *Now that I have told you all the disgusting details of my past. Do you still want me?*

She shouldn't have worried. I still did.

Our third time was slower, less frantic than the first and second. And equally wordless. But before it was because there was no breath for words. Now the silence was due to us having no more words left. At least for a while.

I did not put up as much resistance to her as I had before. It would have been pointless. In Sima Vaaknin's bed I was powerless, and I felt pleasure and guilt mix freely in my body and mind as we tangled and twined deeper into each other.

———

I dozed for a while, and when I woke, she was asleep, curled into herself. I got out of bed and began pulling on my clothes. I must have made a noise, because I heard her voice.

"Leaving?"

She was lying on her back, half covered by the sheets, her skin an appealing contrast to the white of the linen. In the bedroom window, the faint light of the dawning sun was warming the red curtains, casting crimson light about the room.

"Yes. I have work to do today, and I want to get some sleep."

She didn't ask why I couldn't sleep some more in her bed. Perhaps the thought did not cross her mind. I doubted that her clients saw the morning still in her bed, and I wondered what it said about me that I had.

I rummaged in my pocket for money, pulled out what I had, and realized I had not asked her for her price. I looked at her questioningly.

"Whatever you got there," she said, "it doesn't look like enough."

I wasn't sure what to say to that. Finding myself in the position to pay for her favors was awkward enough without feeling like a pauper.

"Leave half of what you're holding, Adam. Consider the rest of my fee paid for by the two broken ribs you gave Maryam's pimp."

I laid the money on her dresser and started buttoning my shirt.

"You will come back again," she said.

I paused, then my fingers started working again. I shook my head. "No. I don't plan to."

"Because you're in love?" she asked, and she didn't ask with whom.

How could I explain to her what it was like, the mixture of love for a dead woman and the guilt that came with feeling you betrayed her? Sima had never felt a love beyond that of a child to his parents and siblings. She had not loved as an adult. And she had not had herself for a lover—desirable beyond resistance, uncompromising between the sheets, all encompassing. Even now my body yearned for her.

And also my mind.

Those few hours with Sima Vaaknin had calmed my mind and erased the aftertaste of my chats with Inspector Rosen and Charlie Buzaglo. But they had left a sediment of guilt and self-loathing in their place. Guilt for Deborah, and self-loathing that I had been weak enough to succumb to Sima Vaaknin's charms so completely.

"Yes," I answered. "Because I'm in love."

A strange light went over her face, or perhaps a strange play of emotion. She appeared contemplative for a fraction of a second and then a grin bloomed on her lips.

"You will come back again," she said. "Your body will not allow you to stay away."

I finished buttoning my shirt, got my shoes on, and slipped on my jacket. I didn't answer her challenge. I simply said goodbye and left.

The streets were bathed in that tentative yellow light of dawn when the sun is making its initial steps toward domination of the sky. It was a time of light traffic, of most people still sleeping, but there were some who had already started their day. Mostly men hurrying to their shops or to catch an early bus for the factory.

When I got to my apartment, I shucked off my clothes and started the water running in the shower. Before stepping under the spray, I paused when I caught the scent of Sima Vaaknin on my skin. Then I got under the water and scrubbed my skin till it was gone.

I went to bed, and in my dreams I saw my wife as she had been, and also as I imagined her last moments must have been. I slept poorly and late and finally got out of bed after three o'clock with the taste of ashes in my mouth. I ate a late lunch and went down to the corner to call Reuben and ask him if he had anything for me regarding Maryam Jamalka's arrest. He told me he had nothing to report. I told him I'd call him again tomorrow and headed to Greta's Café.

I got my chessboard, set up the pieces, and started playing. As I saw it, I had two options: I could wait for Reuben to furnish me with whatever information he could uncover, or I could go find Charlie Buzaglo and have another talk with him, this time in a location that would inspire him with less confidence. Doing the first required me to wait till the next day; doing the latter would be possible later that night.

I stayed at Greta's throughout the afternoon and evening. I read a few of the newspapers left behind by various patrons, ate a little dinner, smoked my cigarettes and wished I had more of Ahmed Jamalka's tobacco. Whenever my mind drifted to Sima Vaaknin, I directed it toward something else. After closing time, I turned over the chairs on the tables and offered to sweep the floor. Greta handed me the broom and went finto the kitchen to make sure everything was in its place.

I worked the room from the back to the front, periodically emptying the pan of dust and dirt, and was more than halfway through when a knock came upon the café's door.

"Adam, can you see who it is?" Greta called from the kitchen.

I answered that I could and went to the door, still clutching the broom.

The man behind the glass was tall and wide, and the darkness of night and lack of illumination masked his face in shadow. I flicked back the bolt and opened the door.

And saw Rafi, Charlie Buzaglo's accomplice on the night they'd attacked me, standing on the threshold.

# 19

I had brought my knife with me to Greta's, but it was in my jacket pocket, and the jacket was draped over the back of the chair I'd occupied throughout the afternoon. That chair was on the far side of the café, well out of reach.

What I did have in my hand was the broom. I started swinging it, aiming to catch Rafi across the head before he could pull out a club or a knife or even a gun.

As I was swinging the broom, two thoughts flashed through my mind. The first was that I couldn't believe Charlie Buzaglo had the guts to send someone to Greta's to attack me—I was sure he wouldn't dare venture out of the streets of Jaffa, where he held the advantage. The second was that Rafi's expression did not seem menacing and that his hands were empty of weapons.

Rafi caught sight of the broom's approach and tried to take a step back to avoid being whacked. He wouldn't have made it—he was too slow on his feet. What saved him was that I arrested the motion of the broom three inches from his head. There we stood on the threshold, two big men, one holding a broom like a weapon, the other with eyes wide and a face drained of blood.

"Whoa, whoa."

Rafi, it appeared, was not articulate when he was nervous or scared.

I lowered the broom. "What are you doing here, Rafi?"

He cast a quick look to both sides. "Can I come in?"

Without turning my back on him, I vacated the doorway. He stepped inside and stuck his hands in his pants pockets.

"Take out your hands," I told him. "Keep them where I can see them."

He took them out and shifted on his feet. I told him to walk to the back. He limped as he walked. I closed and locked the front door. Greta appeared in the entrance to the kitchen.

"Who was it, Adam?" Then she saw Rafi, and her eyebrows rose.

"We're going to have a short talk," I said. I looked at Rafi. "Right?"

He nodded and I told Greta we would need a few minutes of privacy. She nodded and left the room.

Rafi and I went to my table. He dropped into a chair with a grunt. Apparently, being on his feet was uncomfortable with the injury I had given him. I leaned the broom on a neighboring table and slipped my jacket on. Only when I reached into the jacket pocket and felt the comforting shape of my knife did I calm. I could certainly take out Rafi with it, especially with his limp, and there wasn't anyone else here with him.

I stared at him across the table, waiting for him to start talking.

"I thought I would be too late," he said. "I thought this place would be closed."

"It is closed. I was just helping with the sweeping and tidying up."

"Good. If you weren't here, I wouldn't have known where to find you."

"Find me for what?"

"To warn you. They're coming to get you. Charlie's men."

My eyes went to the opening to the kitchen, where Greta was tidying up. "Here?"

"No. To your apartment. Charlie had someone follow you last night after you left the club."

I frowned, recalling that I had listened for sounds that someone was coming out of the club after me and heard none.

"I didn't notice anyone," I said.

"He had a guy on the street, waiting for you to come out, and he trailed you all the way to your place."

"But that would mean…" I started saying but didn't finish the sentence. Because I had already figured out that Charlie Buzaglo had been expecting me. He had known I was looking for him, why else would he be at the nightclub I was bound to check out first?

If I ran, I could get to my apartment in a few minutes. And I had the Luger there, in my box, loaded and ready for action.

If I wanted to face them.

Perhaps avoidance was the best option, but they might trash the apartment, and I didn't want them to take the things in my box. "When are they coming? How many?"

"Soon. They might be heading out as we speak. I was there earlier when Charlie talked to them. He told them to wait until after dark, when they were sure you'd be home. I got away as soon as I could. There are three guys in total, though one may just be the driver."

I still had time. I could be in my apartment and out before they came. I could lie in wait for them or avoid them altogether. Still, wasting time was foolish. I got to my feet. "And what are they supposed to do to me?"

"They're coming to kill you. 'Kill the son of a bitch,' is what

Charlie told them. 'Kick him in the ribs a few times first if you can.' You made him very angry that night."

Good, I thought, and it wouldn't be the last thing I did to Charlie Buzaglo.

Rafi and I walked to the café's entrance, and I called out to Greta that I was leaving.

At the door I asked him, "Why are you here, Rafi? Why warn me?"

"Because of what you did the night we came after you, Charlie and me. Sure, you busted up my knee, but I would have done the same to you and worse. I was sure you were going to kill me that night. And if I had been in your shoes, I'd have done so. I figured I owed you." He shifted his eyes to the side. "And besides, Charlie's been riding me ever since that night, calling me names, telling everyone how clumsy and slow I am. The only reason he had me witness his little talk with the men who are coming for you was so he could make fun of me some more. 'Now you'll see how real men handle business, Rafi.' He shouldn't have made fun of me in front of the others. That wasn't nice. I hope you can pay him back for both of us."

"Don't worry," I said. "I will. But I'll need to find him where I can reach him. Where does he live?"

There was the slightest hesitation, and then he gave me an address deep inside Jaffa.

I told him it would be good if he never told anyone about our meeting.

"Are you kidding?" he said. "If anyone knew I was here, I'd be a dead man, even if Charlie Buzaglo was no longer around to do it himself. This is how it is in my line of work."

I nodded in understanding. "You did good coming here, Rafi. Thank you."

He shrugged. "Now we're even."

"Yes. Now we are."

He walked off one way and I the other, toward home. It took me ten steps before I realized that I was heading for the wrong place. Rafi had told me that Buzaglo had someone follow me home from the nightclub the previous night. But I did not go home from the nightclub. I went to Sima Vaaknin's apartment. And that was not that close to where I was standing now. Charlie's men might get there ahead of me. And they would find Sima...

I started running.

# 20

I pumped my arms, pushing myself hard, feet pounding on the pavement. It was a warm night, and Allenby Street was busy with pedestrians enjoying the nice weather. I weaved my way around people, once having to step into the road to dodge a burly man who was drunk and uneven on his feet. As I stepped off the curb, a car horn blared behind me and brakes shrieked, and I heard the driver shouting after me, questioning my sanity in spicy Yiddish.

People watched with puzzled expressions as I ran past them, and one guy asked half-jokingly if I had done something to upset my wife and had her on my tail. I didn't waste my breath explaining that I was running toward danger, not away from it.

A taxi went by, and I tried to hail it, but either the driver didn't see me, or something about the way I looked made him think he would be better off with some other fare. I kept on running, and a few hundred meters farther north, I noticed another taxi at the curb, discharging a fare. It was a woman in her fifties, gray hair held in a tight bun at the back of her head, and as she paid the driver and bid him goodnight, I grabbed the door she was about to close, and jumped into the car.

The driver was balding, with wide-set brown eyes and a thick nose.

"Sorry, but I'm done for this evening. You need to find yourself another taxi."

I grabbed whatever cash I had in my pocket, held it out to him, and gave him Sima's address. "Get me there in the next five minutes and I won't bother with change."

He eyed the money, then my face, then the money again. He shrugged and said, "All right. Hang on to the door handle."

I did just that and he shot away from the curb. The taxi wasn't built for racing, but he got what he could out of it. He muttered under his breath throughout the drive. The words were Romanian, and he was asking himself whether running into another car or a building was worth the money I'd offered him. All this self-doubt didn't seem to slow him down any or make him less focused on the road ahead. He made his way expertly uptown without incident and turned onto Sima's street after exactly six minutes.

I wasn't about to begrudge him a minute. I handed him the money and got out of the car. He yelled, "Good night," after me as I rushed to Sima's building and up the stairs to her floor. I had glanced up at her window from the street below and saw a light burning behind the curtains. A disturbing mental image of Sima in the arms of a client flashed through my mind and I shoved it away.

I tried her door. It was locked. I pounded on it. My heart was hammering a nasty beat in my chest. The locked door was a good sign, I decided. Maybe I was in time.

Or maybe Charlie Buzaglo's men were inside, hurting Sima as I stood there like an idiot.

I got out my knife, flicked it open, and got myself ready to fight.

A key was turning on the inside of the door. I adjusted my grip on the knife. But it was only Sima, looking lovely in a white-and-red checked dress that went to her ankles. She was grinning at me, her eyes glinting with mischievous triumph.

"I wasn't expecting you so soon, Adam. Don't tell me you ran all the way here."

Then her eyes caught the knife, and her face changed to that of a frightened child. She stepped back from the door, and I said, "Don't worry. I'm not here to hurt you."

She said nothing and took another step backward. I folded the knife and tossed it to her. "Here," I said. "Now you're the one with the power over me."

I entered her apartment and shut the door behind me. There was no one else present but me and her. Sima was looking at me strangely, clutching the folded knife to her chest. She wasn't trembling or gathering her breath to scream. Giving her the knife had broken the initial fear, morphing it into anxious bewilderment.

I explained the situation as succinctly as I could: I'd been followed last night to her apartment by a man working for Charlie Buzaglo. Now three of his men were coming here, to where they thought I lived, to kill me. They could be there at any moment. She had to leave. Right now.

I'd expected a scene. A blunt refusal to leave her home, or recriminations, at the very least. But there was nothing. Just a pause the length of two heartbeats as she took in the information. Wordlessly, Sima handed me my knife back and went down the hall into another room. She came back out in less than a minute. She had pulled back her hair and secured it in place with a clip and slipped on a light black coat and comfortable-looking shoes. A large black bag hung over her shoulder.

"I'm ready," she said.

I stared at her. She didn't have time to pack anything, no clothes or toiletries of any kind. The only way that bag contained what she would need for a few days away from home was if she had packed it in advance. And then I recalled the story she told me yesterday, about the young Sima Vaaknin driven from her home in Hebron and later having to run away from another home, only to land in the clutches of a pimp. Sima Vaaknin had learned that life was unstable and unpredictable, that trouble might come knocking on her door at any moment, that she needed to be ready to run when it did. And I was the cause of this current escape. I had brought danger to her door. The thought made my gorge rise.

"Come," I said, and she exited the apartment without a backward glance.

We made our way down the stairs, me in front, holding the now open knife by my right thigh. With a hand gesture I told her to stop when we reached the entrance hall. There was no car idling at the curb, no headlights shining brighter as they drew nearer to where we stood.

"Let's go," I said, and we crossed the small front yard with quick, light steps. There was a waist-high stone fence at the edge of the yard, and we got down low behind it when we heard footfalls and talking voices approaching on the other side of the street. Sima kept her head down as I peeked over the fence, and I could hear her breathing short, shallow breaths. She was scared. She was trying to hide it, but her rapid breathing gave her emotions away.

The voices belonged to three men, and I tensed as I waited for them to cross over toward us. I would have to jump them, try to get one immediately with a killing slash, and hope that the other two weren't good enough fighters.

But the three men just kept on walking, and when I heard one of them let out a loud, braying sort of laugh, I realized they were just three random guys shooting the breeze, passing the time.

Sima and I got up and started walking down the sidewalk when a pair of headlight beams swung in a wide arc toward us as the car they belonged to turned onto Sima's street.

I grabbed Sima's hand, and we ran hunched over into a neighboring yard. It was also bordered by a fence, and we squatted behind it. The car was coming in slow, like the driver was checking out the building numbers, and I was filled with the certainty that this was them, Buzaglo's men. I peered over the fence and saw that the car was a black Skoda 1101, with its flat, truncated back and its long, snout-like front. The front passenger seat was taken and there were the shadows of two passengers in the backseat.

So there were four men, not three. Buzaglo was taking no chances.

The Skoda, inching along now, was coming up on where Sima and I hid. I was struck by a sudden fear that they might have gotten the number of the building wrong, either last night or right now, and the four of them would come into the yard where Sima and I were.

Sima was crouched beside me, her back to the fence, her bag on the ground at her feet. Her side was touching mine, and I felt a tremor where our bodies connected. I couldn't say who was shaking, me or her, and I kept my eyes firmly on the car. I could hear my breathing now, and it seemed loud and strident. My mind was amplifying the sound, I knew, but it still made me nervous, like the men in the car would be able to hear me over the grumble of the motor.

But the Skoda crept by, coming to a stop just outside Sima's building. The doors flew open and all four men got out. They were all young, two tall and two of average height. One of them held a pistol in his hand, and he quietly jacked a round into its chamber. I could only make out two of their faces by the glow of the nearest streetlight, and I committed them to memory. Their heads turned this way and that as they scanned the street, and I ducked my head, not wanting to risk being spotted. I heard them exchange a few barely audible words—final instructions, I imagined—and then the thud of their shoes on the stone path cutting across the yard of Sima's building.

The sound of their footsteps faded, and I dared another peek. All four men were gone, having climbed the stairs to Sima's apartment. In a moment, they would discover an empty apartment, and then they'd come down. What would happen then was unclear. Either they would go back to Buzaglo to report their failure to find me, or they'd stake out the apartment and street, hoping I'd show up. I expected them to do the latter. If I was right, and we stayed where we were, Sima and I would be unable to leave our hidden position for the rest of the night.

It was time to go.

"We have to move," I said, grabbing her forearm and pulling her to her feet. I took the bag from her, and we ran across the street, through a dark yard, where we roused a few angry cats, who hurled screeches after us that sounded as loud as cannons.

We didn't pause when we reached the parallel street, but crossed it as well, and through another yard to the next street south. There I allowed us to slow to a walk, and we made our way west, both of us gasping for breath.

A few minutes later we came upon a tiny playground with a couple of swings, half a dozen trees, and three benches. We sat on one and I wiped the sweat off my face. Sima alternated between looking at me and at the street, as if sure the four men would suddenly appear there.

"I'm sorry, Sima," I said. "I got you involved in all of this."

"I was already involved," she said. "The moment I took Maryam home with me. And I don't regret it. I would do it again." Her fathomless eyes latched onto mine, and I was stunned to see her lips twitching with the onset of a smile. "I would do it all again, Adam."

The heat of the run was leaving my body, but her words and the way she was looking at me brought another kind of heat in its place. Even scared for her life, she was trying to seduce me.

"What would you have done had they come before me?" I asked. "Do you have a way to defend yourself?"

She shook her head. "Perhaps I should get something."

"That would be a good idea."

"Would it have helped Maryam if she had a weapon?"

"I don't know. A weapon is never enough in and of itself. You need the will to use it and the skill to use it well. But it's not important right now. What's important is that you get out of Tel Aviv for a few days. Do you have a place you can go to?"

"There is a lovely hotel on Mount Carmel, overlooking the bay of Haifa. It's a beautiful place, trees and greenery all around. And quiet. I stayed there a few months ago. I'd planned on going again. Now is as good a time as any."

I remembered that I'd given all the money I had on me to the taxi driver.

"I have no money to give you. I—"

She raised an eyebrow. "I have money of my own, Adam. Don't worry about that."

Of course. She had a bag all ready to go. She'd have money there too.

"What will you do while I'm gone?" she asked.

"Finish this. Find out who killed Maryam."

"And deal with her pimp?"

"That's step number one. Charlie Buzaglo made the biggest mistake of his life when he decided not to heed my warning."

Saying nothing, Sima examined my face, and I wondered what she saw there.

"I'll need the name of your hotel so I can reach you when it's safe to come back."

"Is it ever safe to come back?" she asked, and she wasn't looking at me anymore, but straight ahead into the gloom between the trees.

"It will be this time," I said, taking hold of her chin and turning her head to face me. "And it won't take long. I still don't have all the answers, but I'm close. Charlie Buzaglo wouldn't have sent those men after me if I wasn't."

She nodded and told me the name of the hotel.

We got off the bench and stepped out of the small playground and back onto the street.

"Will you be able to get there tonight?" I asked, as the time was now very late.

"The last bus runs at midnight. I'll catch it. Once in Haifa I'll find a taxi to the hotel. And then I can sleep late in a comfortable bed with clean sheets and the crisp air of the Carmel around me."

We stood facing each other, and for a moment I thought she was about to kiss me. The thought filled me with uneasy desire. I had planned never to see her again, because I knew seeing her would mean succumbing to her, and doing so would prove that my ties to my wife were not as strong as they once were. And the guilt that would follow would be hard to bear.

"Go on," I said. "You have nothing to worry about. They don't know about you."

She nodded. "See you soon, Adam."

"I'll let you know when it's safe to return."

She nodded again, turned and walked off. I watched her till

she rounded the corner. Then I rubbed my face and the back of my neck hard enough to feel the skin burn. I had almost gotten her killed. Now she had to flee. This was partly my fault, but mostly the fault of Charlie Buzaglo. And he was going to pay for it.

# 21

I kept to side streets as I headed south toward home. It wouldn't do to be spotted by Buzaglo's men as they finally gave up on finding me. I kept my eyes open for a black Skoda but saw none. I made it to Hamaccabi Street and there was no Skoda by the curb near my building. I was safe, but who knew for how long. The four men would soon figure out that they were in a woman's apartment. They might think it was the apartment of a lover of mine and that I would show up later that night, but at some point they would go back to Jaffa and report what they'd found. Then Charlie Buzaglo would know that he had sent them to the wrong place.

How long would it take him to find out where I lived?

He would probably send someone to watch Greta's Café tomorrow, and when I didn't show up there, he would come to the conclusion that I'd gone into hiding. Then two things would happen: One, he would use all his contacts to try to figure out where I'd gone and where my real apartment was; and two, he would be worried that I was coming for him.

For now, though, he didn't know that I knew he had sent men

after me. For now, he might not have his full guard up. For now, he might be vulnerable. Especially since I knew where he lived.

Still, my apartment would not be a safe place for much longer. Not while Charlie Buzaglo was a threat to me. And I needed my gun to go after him and some money to pay for a hotel room for the night.

I went up to my place, put my ear to the door, and heard nothing. I went in but didn't turn the lights on. I got my box out of its secret compartment. I took out the gun and all the ammunition I had for it. I always kept it loaded, but I checked that the magazine was full just the same. I stuck the gun in the waistband of my slacks and the rest of my ammunition in one jacket pocket. I grabbed all the money I had in the apartment and put it in the other pocket.

I was hungry, but I didn't dare spend any more time in my apartment than I absolutely had to. I found a taxi on King George Street, but the driver refused to take me deep into Jaffa at this time of night. "I'll only go as far as Hashaon Square," he said.

Once there, I paid the driver and headed south and east into the narrow streets in the heart of Jaffa. The streets were dark and dreary. Shadows crowded at the edges of shop fronts and alleyways. There weren't enough working streetlights here, and those that did work burned too feebly to banish the darkness. It was the bad part of the city, and you couldn't be sure that no one would be hiding beyond the reach of the lights, waiting to jump you. I walked close to the edge of the curb, far from alleys and murky entryways. The streets were deserted apart from a few staggering drunks and a couple of groups of bored teenage boys holding their cigarettes like the American actors they saw on the screen at the local cinema.

Two years ago, war had raged in Jaffa. Not just between Jews and Arabs, but also between Jews and British soldiers. Some of the streets still showed signs of the fighting—bullet holes in outer walls and fences, shrapnel damage to the façade of buildings. Some of the buildings exhibited tentative signs of renewal and rejuvenation. In others, repairs had been done haphazardly, leaving uneven patches of plaster and paint like badly healed wounds.

Charlie Buzaglo lived in a small house on Hasfina Street. I parked myself in a recessed doorway diagonally across the street from his door and made myself ready for a long wait.

While I waited, I ran the events of the day through my mind. If it hadn't been for the warning Rafi had given me, Sima might have been dead right now. Still, it had been a close call, not just for her, but for me as well.

And I hadn't seen it coming. Charlie Buzaglo had surprised me with this escalation. Pimping and smuggling and even the killing of a criminal associate were one thing, sending a team to murder a citizen in the heart of Tel Aviv was another. That could have proved dangerous for him, because the police would vigorously investigate such a killing. They might learn that I had been seen in his company not just once, but twice in the past week. They might ask him some uncomfortable questions.

I stood in that doorway for over two hours, and in that time not a soul passed by in the street. Then I heard the sound of a car approaching, and I took out my Luger and held it by my side. The car was a blue Ford, and there were two men in front and one in back. The car stopped by Buzaglo's building, and the driver opened his door. By the inner light of the car, I could make out his face. He was one of the four men who had come to Sima's building. The man who sat in front beside him also got out, and together they took a cursory look around the street. Their eyes went over the shadowed doorway in which I stood, but they didn't see me. Charlie Buzaglo got out of the backseat, wearing a leather jacket, hands in his pockets.

I was considering how best to take out the two bodyguards when out of the shadows further down the street came the roar of an engine as a car screeched to a halt meters away from Charlie Buzaglo and his men. Two tall men leapt out of the car, their right arms outstretched before them, guns in their hands. The guns flashed like fireworks, and the blast of their reports echoed in the narrow street.

One of Buzaglo's men got it right away. I saw a plume of blood gush out of his throat and drench the front of his shirt. He fell back against the hood of the Ford and slumped down to a sitting position, head lolling on his chest, dead. The next couple of shots smashed into Buzaglo's Ford, punching holes in the side panels, shattering a passenger window. Buzaglo's other man got out his gun and managed to squeeze off one wild shot before getting hit in the leg. He toppled to the road with a shriek of agony, landed hard on his side, and his gun fell from his hand and clattered away from him. Buzaglo was running toward the front door of his building when he got it in the small of his back. He fell down on the sidewalk and tried crawling toward the door.

One of the two attackers walked to the man who was shot in the neck and put another bullet into him. The other one went to where Buzaglo's second guard lay clutching his leg with one hand and shot him in the head, putting an end to his howling. One of the car's headlights fell across the second shooter's swarthy, mustached face. The other one said something to him in Arabic, and I couldn't make out any of the words, apart from the first one, *Kadir*, and I knew that these were the two Jamalka brothers. The two criminals and murderers, who Talmon was certain had murdered their sister, and who Ahmed Jamalka was certain had not.

Buzaglo was grunting in pain, inching his way like a wounded snake toward his building. The two brothers turned their heads toward him. They were about to finish him off. If they did, I would never know what had happened to their sister.

I raised the Luger and fired.

The slug got Kadir Jamalka in the shoulder. He swiveled like a dreidel and fell. Jalal turned in my general direction, mouth gaping in surprise, and fired. He couldn't see where I was, and the bullet went wide. I took aim at him, but he was already moving, dragging his brother behind the cover of their car. He pulled Kadir to his feet and fired again at me over the roof of their vehicle, a wild series of shots that made me duck my head and flatten myself into the doorway. I heard a car door slam and an engine rev and the sound of tires wailing against the tarmac as they tore off. I dared a glance and saw the car slewing round the near corner as they took it at top speed.

The sound of gunfire echoed in my ears like faraway thunder. The air was thick with the smell of spent gunpowder. I started crossing the street and paused when my shoe fell on something hard. It was the shell casing from the Luger. I picked it up, put it in my pocket, and went to where Charlie Buzaglo lay.

He was lying face down, right cheek flat against the sidewalk stones, hands by his head, like a man trying to surrender. Blood was pumping out of his back, and he was groaning softly. I got down beside him and made sure he could see my face.

"Get me to a hospital," he said, the words coming out in wheezy, short exhalations.

"Only if you tell me what happened to Maryam Jamalka," I told him. "If you don't, I'll leave you here to bleed out in the street like a dog."

"You son of a bitch."

I shrugged. "The more time you waste, the more blood you lose. Talk or die. Your choice. Tell me what happened to Maryam Jamalka. What happened on the night she was arrested? Why didn't you take her back? Who killed her?"

Blood was bubbling out of his lips now, and his face was losing color. Oddly, sweat beads sprouted along his forehead. I knew that I had given him a false choice. He was going to die anyway. Even if I got him into the car that very moment and stomped on the gas pedal the whole way to the hospital, he wasn't going to make it. He would die here on this dismal Jaffa street. It bothered me none. If lying to this rat was what I had to do to get to the bottom of this case, then so be it.

He started talking. The story came in fits and bursts between grunts of pain and shaky breaths. I asked him a few questions at first, but then I just let him talk, worrying that he might die on me before I got the whole story. It only took him a couple of minutes to tell me everything he knew, and what he told me filled in most of the gaps in what I had uncovered so far, painted in the blanks in the mental picture I had begun to draw, and added grim color and rough texture and horrible truth.

When he was done, Charlie Buzaglo let out a last faint whimper of air and died. And I knew who had killed Maryam Jamalka.

## 22

I left Buzaglo and his men in the street where they lay and walked quickly away from the scene of the firefight. No neighbors came out to their balconies to see what was going on. No one rushed down from their apartment to offer help. No lights flared in any of the windows. I could understand that. It was better to keep one's head down, to hope that the bullets didn't find their way into your bedroom. It was better to keep your eyes averted, because becoming a witness might place you in danger, might make you a target.

Still, someone would call the police eventually. Or someone's curiosity would get the better of them and they would take a peek out their window. I wanted to be long gone by then.

I walked with my head down till I was a few streets away. Then I leaned against a low fence and let myself rest for a few minutes as the last dregs of adrenaline faded from my bloodstream. I was shaking, and my body was tired, craving to lie down and get some sleep. I put a cigarette between my lips and started walking again. I kept on walking till I got out of Jaffa and into Tel Aviv.

Near the southern tip of Hayarkon Street, I found a hotel. It wasn't much, though with a cleaner and better-looking façade than the Jaffa Star Hotel, where Maryam Jamalka used to take her clients. I registered under a false name and got a second-floor room.

The room was small. A bed, one nightstand, a tiny wash-room, a tall and narrow closet with two hangers in it. But it was clean and tidy and smelled fresh, and the window looked on the Mediterranean.

I stood by the window for some minutes, watching the reflection of the moon and stars on the rolling and shifting surface of the sea. The smell of salt and seaweed was thick in the night air, the whisper of gently breaking waves soothing. I kept the window open, laid my Luger and knife within easy reach on the nightstand, took off all my clothes, and slipped into bed. I fell asleep within minutes and slept the rest of the night through without dreams.

I woke after nine o'clock, feeling refreshed but hungry, went down to the street, and picked up a newspaper. The shooting in Jaffa was front-page news. The headline blared the body count, and the article lamented the sordid conditions in certain parts of Jaffa and the crime that was rife there. The article ended with an exhortation for the police to take harsher measures to bring about law and order to the areas in question. The article did not mention the names of the three dead men, nor did it provide any details as to the firefight that claimed their lives. The police had commented, saying that a full investigation had been launched and that the culprits would soon be apprehended. They made sure to mention that all three victims had a criminal record. This was done to calm the general public, to give the impression that such things only happened among criminals, never to law-abiding citizens.

In a nearby café, I had a small but adequate breakfast of

bread and cheese and coffee. The proprietor tried to engage me in conversation about last night's shooting. I nodded in all the right places until he got bored of me and went to talk to someone else.

The café had a telephone and I placed a call to Reuben. He was not at his desk and I declined to leave a message with the officer who answered the call.

Half an hour later I called Reuben again, and this time I was in luck. He asked me if I'd read the newspapers about the three men shot to death in Jaffa, and I told him I had.

"It's like one of those Mafia movies," he said, and I agreed that it was. I felt bad about keeping information from him, but the way the case was shaping up, I doubted that it would have the sort of law-and-order ending that Reuben would feel comfortable with.

I asked him if he'd found anything worth noting about the three days Maryam Jamalka had spent in jail.

"It seems perfectly routine," he said. "She didn't make trouble, no fights with other inmates, no special requests. But I did find something intriguing when I asked one of the guards to check out the visitors' log." I wasn't surprised by the name he gave me, though I acted as if I was.

"What does this mean, Adam?" he asked me.

"It means that you need to be very careful, Reuben. Don't ask any more questions. Let it go for now."

"And you?"

"I'll be careful too."

Next I called the contact number Ahmed Jamalka had given me the day we met. The person who answered the phone had the voice of an old man who had smoked most of his life and a thick Arabic accent. But he knew Hebrew well enough. He told me he could pass on a message to Ahmed, and I asked him to tell

Ahmed to be by the phone in two hours and that I had important information for him.

I went back to my hotel room and lay down for an hour and a half, thinking and planning, before heading out to call Ahmed Jamalka once more.

"Can you come over to Tel Aviv tomorrow?" I asked when I had him on the line.

"What for?"

"So I can tell you who killed your sister."

There was a pause. "I already know who killed her," he said.

"No. You just think you do. How is your brother, by the way? Is he hurt bad?"

There was a sharp intake of breath. "You? It was you?"

"Yes. Your brothers killed the wrong man last night. Well, allow me to amend that, he certainly deserved dying, but he did not kill Maryam."

"Explain."

"Not on the phone. You want to hear this in person. Can you come?"

"Yes," he said. "I can come."

We settled on ten o'clock the following morning and arranged to meet at Gan Meir, a park at the center of Tel Aviv.

"I want you to ask your brothers a few things for me," I told him.

"What things?"

I told him what I wanted him to ask them. He asked me why I wished to know these things, and I told him that it would help me prove to him who had murdered Maryam.

Then I told him to bring something along with him. And there was another pause and he asked me why.

"I'll tell you tomorrow. Just be sure to have it with you."

I ended the call and took a minute to think things through, to make sure I had gotten everything straight in my mind. Then I picked up the phone and rang another number, and fifteen minutes later, I had set up another meeting for the next day. Time: eleven thirty. Place: to be determined half an hour before that.

# 23

I called him at eleven o'clock, gave him the location for the meeting, and told him to come alone and on foot.

It was a hot day and he grumbled a bit over being made to walk. I told him he could either do as I said, or the meeting was off. "Fine," he said. "We'll do it your way."

I would be watching him, I told him. If he tried to play games with me, I would be gone and our deal would be off.

I took up position in a café on King George Street and watched as he made his way north and turned into Gan Meir. He was alone and punctual. The time was precisely eleven thirty.

Gan Meir was a public park in the dead center of Tel Aviv, bordered by King George Street to the east and Tchernichovski Street to the west. Never without people during the day, it was the perfect place for this meeting. Plenty of witnesses.

He took the bench I'd instructed him to take, the fourth one on the left side by the big lawn with the water fountain at its center. I followed him in and sat down beside him. The sun shone straight down from its zenith, but the bench was shaded by a looming ficus tree. He smelled of some cologne that irritated my nostrils. There was also that rich smell I remembered from last time. But now I knew what it was.

He straightened the seam of his perfectly pressed uniform pants and wiped a speck of dirt or lint from his breast pocket. He removed his cap, set it on one knee, and drummed on it with two fingers while a young mother pushing a baby carriage walked by the bench.

"I don't appreciate being dragged out of my office in the middle of the day like this," he said once the mother was out of earshot. "And I don't like walking when I have a perfectly good car I can use."

"Yet here you are," I said.

"Yes. But only because you made it clear that after this conversation you will cease your investigation into Maryam Jamalka's death. I trust that wasn't some ruse on your part."

"No ruse. Once you and I part ways today, I'm done with the case."

"Good. I must admit I was surprised to get your call. I thought you wouldn't back off without some harsh measures on my part. You struck me as the bullheaded sort that doesn't see reason unless it is shown to him the hard way."

"Like Charlie Buzaglo was shown reason the hard way?"

His flat gray eyes narrowed for an instant. "I don't believe I know the name."

"That's strange. He told me you two met about three weeks before Maryam Jamalka died."

"Would he care to make a formal statement to that effect?"

"As you very well know, Charlie Buzaglo won't be making any statements. He is dead. He was gunned down with two other men last night in Jaffa. We had a short chat as he lay dying in the street. He told me everything."

Inspector Rosen sucked in his breath. It made a faint whistling sound as the air passed through his teeth. His left eyebrow twitched. He scratched his cheek and ran a forefinger across his mustache, as if to make sure it was still perfectly aligned with the corners of his mouth.

"Well, if the man's dead, then how can I or anyone else know for sure what he told you? If indeed he told you anything in the first place. And even if he were alive to speak his mind, who would have believed such a criminal?"

"I thought you said you didn't know who he was," I said.

Rosen's cheeks turned a little red. He looked around us. There was no one within earshot and I had no recording instrument with me. He relaxed and his lips curled in a smile that died somewhere on the way to his eyes.

"I recalled the name from the police reports that came in last night and this morning regarding the shooting in Jaffa. But pray tell, what did the estimable Mr. Buzaglo share with you as he lay dying in the street?"

"He told me of the night Maryam Jamalka was arrested. He went after the arresting officer and tried to slip him some money so he would let her go. This is what usually happens with this sort of arrest—the officer gets paid off, either with cash or with some intimate time with the prostitute. This time, though, the policeman couldn't be paid off. He had orders to bring Maryam in. Orders from high up. Orders from you."

"From me? Did the arresting officer tell you that?"

"I didn't bother asking him. The chances that he would tell me anything about it are zero. I'm certain you made sure of that. But Charlie Buzaglo tried to get Maryam out all the same. He was Maryam's pimp. She made a lot of money for him. While she was in jail, she wasn't earning. That was when you had a talk with him."

"And what am I supposed to have told him?" Rosen asked.

"You told him to back off, that from now on he was no longer Maryam's pimp, that she belonged to you. You warned him never to talk to her again or be seen with her. Otherwise, you would make trouble for him. You like to use your power to threaten people to do your bidding. Just like you threatened me. But Buzaglo was even more vulnerable to you than I am, because he was a criminal. He couldn't have the police look too hard into his affairs. It would have destroyed him. So he cut his losses and gave up Maryam. It wasn't too hard. It's not like he was in love with her, not like she was with him." I paused, rubbing at my forehead behind which a dull ache blossomed. "It's strange, isn't it, Rosen, the people we fall in love with or become obsessed about. Here was this beautiful girl falling desperately in love with a rat-faced lowlife, and there was you, becoming obsessed with this young girl whom you were charged with locating and delivering to her death."

He stared at me with his flat, emotionless eyes. After a moment he said, "Why are you telling me all of this? Do you really think you can pin this on me?"

"No. I suffer no such illusions. I know what happened, most of it, anyway, but I can't prove a thing."

"In that case, I think it's time we concluded our talk. I gotta tell you, Lapid, you are a strange man. Did you make me walk all the way from headquarters just to hear you utter this nonsense?"

"No. I brought you here because I have one condition for stopping my investigation."

His face hardened. "You're in no position to make demands. As you said, you have nothing on me."

"Not yet, but if I keep digging, who knows what will turn up."

"Keep digging and it might be a hole for yourself that you'll end up with."

"Relax, Rosen. I meant what I said, I'm off the case once this conversation is over. But I have to know."

"Know what?"

"Know everything that happened with Maryam. I know most

of it, but there are small gaps that only you can fill. Do that for me, and you never have to worry about me again."

He looked at me for a moment, forehead furrowed. "You're insane."

"Come on. I think you want to tell me. You're dying to tell someone, and you have no one to tell it to. You've looked around; there is no one who can hear us. There is no risk on your part. But I have to know."

"I'm not telling you anything. Your little theory is just that, a theory. A figment of your imagination."

"Let me tell you what I do know," I said. "I know you work closely with the Jamalka brothers. They need you because it's not so easy for an Arab to move about these days, especially someone with a criminal record, especially when they're moving contraband. You help them move product in and out of Tel Aviv. You give them and their associates in Jaffa police protection. And they pay you handsomely for it."

"Nonsense."

"I can smell it on you," I said, and looked him straight in the eye. "On your breath. That rich smell of tobacco. I smelled it when you came to Greta's Café to threaten me, but I couldn't place it then. When Charlie Buzaglo told me all he knew, the memory came to me—it's a special tobacco from Lebanon. You can't get it in Israel these days, not unless you have special contacts in Beirut. The Jamalka family has such contacts. I should know. Ahmed Jamalka gave me a couple of cigarettes with the same tobacco when he hired me to find out who butchered his sister."

Rosen cursed under his breath. I'm not sure he even noticed it. There were dark thoughts roiling through his mind, but I didn't waste my time trying to guess what they were.

At length he said, "That's hardly proof."

"No," I agreed. "Not even close."

"And neither brother will testify against me. So you still have nothing."

"You're right. I don't. But I can still make trouble for you. I can pass on what I know to Ahmed Jamalka and he may pass it on to his brothers."

"Do you think they care about Maryam being dead?"

"No. But that's not all you did to her. And they might care about that. I will tell them nothing as long as you tell me everything."

He said nothing. His hands were in his lap, and they had both bunched into tight fists. I had no doubt that, at that very moment, he was plotting how to have me killed.

At length he said, "It's a deal. Tell me the rest of what you already know, and I'll fill in the details."

"I know that when Maryam Jamalka fled from home, her brothers were anxious to find her. She had blemished their family honor. They had marked her for death. But they didn't know where she was. Until someone spotted her. Some local Arab in Jaffa saw her on the street. He passed on the word to Jalal and Kadir that he thought Maryam was in Tel Aviv. But he didn't know where she lived, so the brothers came to you for help. They wanted you to find Maryam for them. And you agreed. Am I right so far?"

He gave a curt nod.

"What were you going to do when you found her, just hand her over to her brothers to be killed?"

"Yes. That's what they wanted, and why should I care? It's the way they do things, the stupid Arabs. It's their fault she became a prostitute in the first place. If they hadn't made her run away, she would still be in their village where she belonged."

"And alive," I said.

"And alive."

"But you changed your mind. What happened?"

"I heard she was finding johns in Club Adom, and I went over there one night just to make sure it was really her. I don't know what came over me, but I had to have her. And not just once. It seemed easy enough. Jalal and Kadir were in the north, and they were counting on me to find their sister for them. I could string them along for a while."

"And they also gave you the perfect way to control Maryam, to threaten her."

"Yes. That's why I had her arrested and jailed, to make sure she knew who was in control, so I could put some fear into her."

"That's why you went to visit her in jail," I said, my stomach filling with acid as I considered how Maryam Jamalka must have felt to have this maniac threaten her in her cell.

"That's right. All I had to do was tell her that if she didn't do what I said, I would hand her over to her brothers. She was terrified of them. She would do anything to avoid that. Jalal and Kadir, they can be quite brutal. They like killing. They would have done horrible things to her just so no other female in their family would start entertaining any thoughts of independence from their control."

"Then what happened?"

"She became mine. It was a sweet time. Too short, in the end, but sweet nonetheless. Unfortunately, it couldn't last. Jalal and Kadir were pressuring me, asking what was taking so long, when was I going to find Maryam. I couldn't hide her forever, and I couldn't hand her over to them. She might tell them about me before they killed her. And sooner or later, someone would have seen her and reported it to them. I had to get rid of her." He sighed. "It was the hardest thing I ever did. But I had no choice."

His tone had taken on a mournful edge, and his eyes dropped to his lap. I stared at him. He was actually looking for sympathy. This lunatic who exploited and knifed a young woman.

"You stabbed her," I said.

"Yes."

"More than once."

"A few times. I had to make sure she died."

"And then you cut her face and legs."

"Yes," he said, his voice distant, as if he were reliving the moment.

"Why?"

He didn't answer for a moment. And when he did, it was not the answer I had expected. I thought he mutilated her body so that if it were found, suspicion would fall on her family.

What he said was, "I'm not sure. I just started doing it, and I found that I enjoyed it, so I kept on doing it for a while."

"Was she alive when you cut her like that?"

He turned to me, and his eyes were wistful when he said, "Maybe just in the beginning. You see, I slashed her neck early on. She bled out too fast."

There was a lump in my throat the temperature of ice and the hardness of rock. I had to swallow a few times to get rid of it.

It took me a moment to regain my speech. "And then you dumped her in the Yarkon."

"Yes. I figured either way I was doing the smart thing. If she got washed out to sea, I was in the clear; if she were found, I could tell Jalal and Kadir that she was dead and get them off my back. I wasn't worried about the police. I could control the investigation. Kill it while it was still young. But I didn't figure on that pissant third brother of hers hiring a detective. You know, you caused me a whole lot of trouble. If you'd just left well enough alone, those three men in Jaffa would still be alive."

"How did that happen?"

"You were sniffing around, asking questions, not heeding my warning like you should have done. And then Charlie Buzaglo called me, said you were asking around for him, and wondered what to do if you came to him."

"What did you tell him?" I asked, knowing the answer. Rosen had given Buzaglo the go-ahead to kill me. That was why Buzaglo had dared sending a team after me to Sima's place, where he thought I lived. He had Rosen to cover for him.

"That's not important anymore," Rosen said. "Buzaglo is dead."

"That he is. You arranged it. Once Buzaglo told you I had come asking questions, you sent the Jamalka brothers to eliminate him. What did you tell them, that he was her pimp? That he had killed her? That was smart of you. You wanted him out of the way so I couldn't speak with him. Without him, there can be no case against you. The poor idiot didn't understand he was signing his own death warrant when he told you I'd come to see him."

Rosen shrugged. "Who cares about someone like Charlie Buzaglo? He was scum. And who cares about Maryam Jamalka? She was a cheap prostitute and would have been killed by her family sooner or later." He looked at me. "Why did you keep on digging even when I made it clear there would be a heavy price to pay?"

I didn't answer. He wouldn't have understood. There was something missing in his soul, and I wouldn't be able to fill it with mere words.

After a minute in which I said nothing, he got to his feet and said, "So now you know everything. And I expect you to keep to your word. If you don't, if you keep on working on this case in any way, I will come after you with everything I've got. And after your friends as well."

It was an empty promise. He wanted to lull me, to get me to go back home and let my guard down. Then he would have me killed. He wasn't the sort to leave loose ends.

"Like I said," I assured him, "I am off this case from this moment on. You have my word."

"Good."

He got to his feet and started turning away, when I stopped him by saying I had just one more question.

"What?" he asked, his voice gruff and impatient.

"The reason you gave Talmon about the authorities not wanting to get into a fight with the Jamalka clan, was it true or did you make it all up?"

He smiled thinly. "It's true. Why do you think they've been allowed to run their smuggling operation for so long?"

"Yes, but did that protection extend to murder? Did your superiors know about that?"

"I think it's better if you don't know the answer to that. Are we done?"

"Yes," I said. "We're done."

"Good. And remember, I'll be watching you."

He put on his cap, adjusting it on his head so it sat perfectly centered. He looked like the perfect policeman—tall, masculine, strong, and neat. He turned on his heel and strode toward the King George Street exit. I stayed on the bench.

Across the big lawn, a man lowered the newspaper he had held before his face throughout my talk with Rosen. He folded the paper, tucked it under his arm, and walked after Rosen. I could see the scar on his cheek from where I sat.

I walked off in the opposite direction, away from what was about to happen.

# 24

An hour and a half before my meeting with Rosen, I had waited on another bench in Gan Meir for Ahmed Jamalka to arrive.

He wore a dark jacket over khaki slacks and a white shirt. In the glaring light of the sun, the scar on his cheek stood out like a careless brushstroke of red.

His face showed new lines of fatigue and tension. Gone was the defiant man I had met mere days ago. Now he appeared worn and deflated. He sat looking about him at the people strolling through the park, his face stony, not showing much emotion.

"Did you talk to your brothers?" I asked.

"Yes."

"And what did they say?"

"They confirmed what you told me. Inspector Rosen is their partner in the Tel Aviv police department. They've been in business together for over two years now. After they heard that Maryam was in Tel Aviv, they asked him to locate her for them."

"Did he tell them what she'd been doing in the city?"

"Two days ago." His hands shook as he spoke the words. "He

told them she had been selling her body and that he had the name and address of her pimp, the man who killed her."

"Charlie Buzaglo."

"Yes."

"And they went to Jaffa to kill him."

"Yes. And you're telling me he wasn't her pimp and he didn't kill her."

"Yes and no," I said. "He was her pimp, but the person who killed her was Inspector Rosen."

I told Ahmed about the investigation I'd been running, about tracking down where his sister had lived and where she got most of her clients. I told him about her becoming involved with Charlie Buzaglo and how he had taken advantage of her. Then I told him about my talk with Buzaglo as he lay bleeding out in the street. I related what he told me about Rosen and how I figured out the connection between Rosen and Ahmed's brothers.

Throughout my narration, he kept quiet, alternately looking down at his knees or ahead at nothing in particular.

When I was done, he took a deep breath and said, "Jalal and Kadir asked me where my questions were coming from, and I told them I had hired a private investigator to discover who murdered Maryam. They laughed at me, stunned that I would pay good money on such a pointless endeavor. To them Maryam was of no importance. The only thing they cared about was the family's honor. They wanted to punish her pimp for aiding in her degradation, not her killer for ending her life. And I let them run her off from home." He removed his glasses and put his face in his hands, but not before I noticed that his eyes had gone moist. "If I had been there for her when she asked for my help," he said, "I could have saved her, couldn't I?"

He was right, of course. He was guilty of abandoning his sister to a world she could not handle by herself. A world where she was vulnerable. If he had been a brother to her, by deed and not just by blood, she would still be alive today. I thought all that but said none of it. A moment of stillness passed between us. I broke it by reaching into my pocket and drawing out the two pictures of Maryam he'd given me.

"Here. You'll want these."

He took them in his hands and gazed at them for a long moment. It felt odd to part with them after carrying them for the past eight days. I'd grown attached to this hopelessly romantic dead girl.

Ahmed let out a long breath, slipped the pictures of his dead sister into his jacket pocket, and said, "What happens now?"

"What happens now is that I am meeting Rosen right here at eleven thirty. Did you bring what I told you?"

He turned his eyes to me, and for an instant what I was seeing were his sister's eyes, as they had been captured in the photo he'd given me. And then the defiance came back. He nodded and showed me the knife he had hidden under his jacket.

"A gun would have been better," I said.

He shook his head. "No. It has to be a knife. I'll do to him what he did to her."

I didn't bother telling him he could never do to Rosen all that he did to Maryam. It was something I learned while hunting Nazis after the war. Sometimes you took whatever revenge you could find.

"When we first met," he said, "I told you I wanted to avenge my sister's death. You told me no. You wanted her killer to stand trial. What changed your mind?"

"Reality did," I said. "I know what happened, but I have very little evidence. Buzaglo is dead, and there are no other witnesses who can testify as to the nature of Rosen's relationship with Maryam. What there is won't be enough for an investigation, let alone a conviction."

And in the meantime, Rosen would do anything he could to

stop me. He would send other people to kill me, just as he had sent Jalal and Kadir Jamalka to kill Buzaglo. And I wouldn't be the only one to die. Any potential witness against him would also be killed. In fact, I suspected that Rosen would do that anyway. He would spare no one who might incriminate him.

"I want justice for your sister, and this is the only way to get it."

"Thank you," he said.

I looked at him. "You know what doing this will mean for you? Once you kill Rosen, the police will not rest until you're in custody. You will have to run away, leave Israel."

"I know."

"You won't be able to come back. Ever."

He offered a frail half smile. "Maybe I'll come back as part of an Arab army."

"Then I'll be there to fight you as part of a Jewish one."

His eyes narrowed thoughtfully, and he offered a small nod.

"Just in case you're not able to get away—"

"I will not give the police your name," he said. "You have my word. I owe you my thanks for the work you did for me, and for Maryam."

"I only did what you paid me to do," I said.

"Speaking of which, do I owe you anything?"

"No. The retainer you gave me covers my work. But if you have some of that tobacco…"

He laughed, reached into his pocket, and drew out the tobacco pouch. He handed it to me.

"Take it all. Where I'm going, I can get more with no trouble."

I put the tobacco in my pocket and offered him my hand. He shook it, and I told him where to wait for my meeting with Rosen.

———

What happened after Rosen and I parted company I know only from news reports and what facts I could later gather.

Rosen walked out of Gan Meir and made his way south back to police headquarters. Ahmed followed him by car, passing him and parking some distance ahead on King George. He waited for Rosen to walk by the car, got out, and came up behind him, the knife in his hand covered by the same newspaper he had been reading in the park.

It was unclear precisely what Ahmed shouted as he yanked off the newspaper and plunged the knife into Rosen's back. It was in Arabic, and only a handful of the people who witnessed the stabbing spoke the language with any degree of fluency. But more than one of them recalled hearing the name Maryam even as Ahmed stabbed the now fallen Rosen a second and third and fourth time.

One man rushed Ahmed and tried to disarm him. Ahmed pushed him off but did not try to stab him. He waved the knife around, warning the crowd of people to keep their distance. Then he jumped into his car and tore off.

The police were telephoned from a nearby café, and a doctor who had been walking on the opposite sidewalk at the time of the stabbing attempted to save Rosen's life. But one of the knife thrusts had found his heart, and he died before the ambulance arrived.

It didn't take long for the police to identify Ahmed. Often, in such attacks, what people remembered could be hazy and lacking in detail. But this time there was no such problem. Everyone recalled Ahmed's scar. One woman said it was so red, she thought he was bleeding.

I was in Greta's Café, drinking scalding coffee when one of the regulars burst in, excitement coloring his face, and informed the rest of the patrons of what had happened on King George Street.

"Stabbed him in the back," he said. "The coward. Just stabbed him and left him to die in the street."

There were some nasty comments among the regulars. And one man predicted that it was the opening shot of a new war with the Arabs. Greta looked shaken, and that was the only thing about Rosen's death that made me sad.

# 25

Two days later, Yossi Talmon stomped his way to my table at Greta's and stood there glowering at me. His eyes were no longer sad. Now they looked furious.

"Good morning, Yossi," I said.

"You lunatic," he said through gritted teeth. "Do you have any idea what you've done?"

I made a show of looking around. "Sit down, Yossi. You're attracting attention."

For a moment he just stood there, and I could see his upper lip twitching, making his mustache dance. Then he planted himself in a chair opposite me. He sat there glaring at me, his entire face set as if it had been carved in stone. He looked a little like a mad bear, with his bushy beard and mustache and angry eyes. He looked about ready to maul me.

Greta's eyes had followed Talmon's march toward my table. She had risen out of her chair by the window and was now leaning on the counter, looking our way, a worried frown on her face. I smiled reassuringly at her.

To Talmon I said, "I'm assuming this is about Rosen."

"What else could it be about? Please tell me you did not give Ahmed Jamalka the idea that Rosen killed his sister."

"It happens to be the truth."

His eyes nearly popped out of his head. A vein in his temple throbbed. "You'd better explain that, Adam," he said.

I told him everything, how I took his advice and started with Maryam Jamalka's criminal record, how it led me to Club Adom, and from there to where she lived and the hotel to which she took clients. I explained how I'd learned that Charlie Buzaglo had been Maryam's pimp and how he had tried to have me killed. I described how I'd waited outside his home, saw him and his men get gunned down in the street, and the talk I had with him before he died. Finally, I gave an account of my talk with Rosen in Gan Meir.

During my narration, Talmon's expression morphed from anger to incredulity to reluctant belief, the latter when I told him about Rosen's visit to Maryam Jamalka while she was in jail. He kept tugging and pulling so hard at his beard that I expected it to come out in tufts.

When I was finally done, Talmon stared at me in silence for a few moments. Then he said, "So you sent Ahmed Jamalka to kill Rosen."

"I told him the truth," I said, "but I did not send him to kill Rosen. He did that all by himself."

"But you knew he would do it, didn't you?"

"Yes. Though my answer would be different if this were an official investigation. Is it?"

"It isn't and you know it. If it were, you'd be sitting in a windowless interrogation room instead of this sunny café. But it might become official in the very near future, don't think it won't."

"I will think no such thing, Yossi. Though I can't see what the charge would be—telling person A that person B killed person A's sister is hardly a crime, when it's the truth. And I fail to see what you're so upset about. You wanted justice for Maryam Jamalka, and now you have it."

"Goddamn you, you know I didn't want it this way. This may be the way you did things in Hungary, but it's not the way we do them here in Israel."

"And how do you do things in Israel?" I asked.

"In Israel we put people on trial, and when they're found guilty, we lock them up in prison."

"Does this include cases the police decide not to investigate? Because in Hungary such cases never made it to trial."

He blinked, then slumped a bit in his chair, looking at me with eyes that shone a tad less with anger and a tad more with sadness.

"You son of a bitch," he said, in a low voice. "This is not how I wanted things to go. When I gave you that file, I told you I wanted you to go to the press with proof, and then the department would have been forced to act on it."

"Yes. I know what you wanted. That was back when you thought the killers were Jalal and Kadir Jamalka." I paused, softening my tone. "Look, Yossi, if I had found conclusive, irrefutable proof, I would have gone to the press. But what I had wasn't nearly enough for court, and you know it. And it wouldn't have been enough for the press either. Especially not when a police inspector is involved. And Rosen already knew I was onto him. One of these days, he would have gone after me. I wasn't about to let him do that."

"So you had Ahmed Jamalka do your dirty work for you."

"I let him deliver the justice you and I couldn't. Or wouldn't." I stared at Talmon levelly, and at length he averted his eyes.

"Ahmed Jamalka was my client. He paid me to find out who killed his sister. What I did was my job. What he did was his business, not mine. And I know it's not the sort of justice you had in mind, but it's close. Rosen won't be killing anyone else. And that's what counts."

He glared at me for a while longer before his eyes went to my glass. "Is that coffee you have there?" he asked.

"Yes."

"Is it good?"

"The best in Tel Aviv. Let me get you a cup."

I went to the counter, where Greta sat watching.

"You keep getting visitors who seem intent on punching your lights out," she said.

"Uh-huh. But they all calm down pretty quickly, don't they?"

"Yes, you're a regular tranquilizer. But I wish they'd come in here calm to begin with, because seeing them all upset does very little good for my nerves."

"I'm sorry about that, Greta. Can I get some coffee for my new calm friend?"

She nodded and poured me a cup.

I walked back to the table and handed it to Talmon.

"Thank you." He took a sip and sighed. "You're still a son of a bitch, but this is good coffee. I'll grant you that."

"You're welcome."

He took another sip and tugged gently at his beard. He peered at me. "If I'd known how this would turn out when I agreed to meet you that night in Holon…"

"Then what? You wouldn't change a thing. Not now when you know what kind of madman Rosen was."

He sighed, pulled some more at his beard, and nodded. "No. I guess I wouldn't. All things considered."

"And you haven't considered everything."

"What do you mean?"

"Tell me, Yossi, what is the mood like in the police station?"

"The mood?"

"Regarding Rosen's killing, how are the men taking it?"

"How do you think? It's not every day that a policeman is killed in Israel. And you know how it goes—there's a bond between policemen. If one of us gets it, we won't rest until his killer is caught. If your client was still in the country, he would either be in jail, with some broken bones, or in the morgue."

"I assume this sentiment goes all the way to the top."

"Of course. Rosen was an inspector, after all. He was in command, however low, and that makes it almost personal to the higher-ups." He gave me a thoughtful look. "What are you driving at?"

"It just made me think, that's all, that the unofficial immunity given to the Jamalka brothers, Jalal and Kadir, may be ripe for revocation."

Talmon's eyes widened. His mouth dropped open a bit. "My God. You have thought this through, haven't you, Adam? Tell me, is getting your client's brothers arrested also part of your job?"

"No. But no client of mine buys immunity for his criminal siblings. In addition, I happen to agree with you that murderers in Israel belong in jail, political expediency be damned. And Jalal and Kadir Jamalka are murderers, are they not?"

"That they are," Talmon said. He narrowed his eyes at me. "Not that we can prove it. Of course, since you saw them shoot Charlie Buzaglo, now we can."

"I don't see myself testifying to that effect in court. My memory is hazy on the issue. However, there are other crimes that they committed for which there is proof. Enough for you to lock them up for a good many years. Right?"

"No doubt about that. It won't be the same as convicting

them of murder, but—" he smiled a faint smile "—it will be close."

I watched as the last drops of tension and anger drained from his body. He didn't look happy, perhaps that was beyond the reach of his features, but he seemed satisfied. He finished his coffee.

"This is good coffee. I think I'd like another one. Want one more, Adam?"

I said that I would. He went and fetched it.

When he came back to the table, he said, "Why don't you join the police force, Adam? I'd be happy to put in a word. A man like you, I dare say you could go far."

"No offense, Yossi, but no thanks."

"Why? You practically do the same thing we do."

Not exactly, I thought. What I said was, "I don't like having anyone tell me what to do. And what I can't do."

He pursed his lips, staring intently at his coffee cup. Finally, he said, "I did what I could for her, Adam."

"I know you did, Yossi. You're a good man. You did more than most. We wouldn't be sitting here if you hadn't."

He took a long sip of his coffee, smacked his lips. "You know, last night, after I heard that Rosen was dead, was the first night of good sleep I've had since he ordered me to back off from the case. No dreams of any kind."

I said nothing.

"I guess I should thank you for that," he said.

"No need."

"For a while there," he said, seeming not to have heard me, "I thought I would never sleep properly again."

I didn't say anything. I knew how he felt. Only what he'd gone through for a month, I had been dealing with for five years. And I doubted that would change any time soon.

We talked for a while longer. Our conversation drifted to

other matters, mundane stuff, and I enjoyed speaking with him. I'd been sincere when I said he was a good man. I did not judge him. As he told me the first time we met, he had a family to feed and take care of. That changed a man and the way he did things. I had no one, so it was easier for me to take risks. Still, I'd like to think that in his shoes I would have stayed on the case even if a superior ordered me not to. Murder was special. It didn't let go of you. It demanded resolution and justice. And retribution. I would have felt compelled to deliver all three.

A while later he said, "It's funny."

"What is?"

"How everything ends up so tidy."

"What do you mean?"

"Not only does Rosen get knifed in the street, but also Buzaglo, Maryam's pimp, ends up dead. And now the two brothers will get their just punishment. All the people who wronged Maryam Jamalka are paying the price for their sins toward her."

"That's good," I said. "I hate loose ends."

———

I wasn't sure what to tell Reuben. He was a by-the-book sort of policeman and person. He wouldn't understand that sometimes you had to bend the rules to bring about justice.

But he had questions, as he had known about Rosen's involvement in the case and had heard the reports of what Ahmed Jamalka had shouted as he knifed Rosen in the street.

He asked me what I made of it all, and I gave him an almost complete version of the truth. I described the course of my investigation, leaving out my involvement with Sima Vaaknin and my telling Ahmed Jamalka that Rosen was the killer. This, I suggested, he had managed to learn all by himself.

Reuben was silent for a while on the phone, and I began

worrying that he saw through my lie. At last he said, "I don't like vigilantism. If men started taking the law into their own hands, what kind of society would we have?"

The kind that had always existed, I thought, in which laws were malleable tools of the powerful. But I said nothing.

"But in this case," Reuben went on, "what I hate more is the fact that no one will know the truth. That bothers me."

I told him it bothered me as well, though it barely did. Making the truth public was less important to me than bringing a killer to justice. That it was a justice administered by Ahmed Jamalka and not a black-robed judge in Tel Aviv bothered me even less.

Three days later, around ten o'clock in the morning, I bought that morning's issue of *Davar* from a kiosk on Rothschild Boulevard and sat reading it on a street bench around which pigeons scoured for bread crumbs.

There was a story on page 2 with the following headline: "A Police Shoot-out in the Galilee Leaves Two Men Dead and One Wounded."

The story described a police operation in an Arab village in the Galilee. The culprits were two brothers, Jalal and Kadir Jamalka. Both men were said to possess a lengthy career in crime, with sins ranging from petty theft to extortion and assault. Much worse was hinted at. The two brothers were also said to have fought against Israel in the War of Independence and to have continued their life of crime since the war had ended. Their brother was Ahmed Jamalka, the man who had stabbed to death police inspector Avi Rosen just a few days earlier in Tel Aviv and was believed to have fled the country to an enemy nation. The picture the report painted was crystal clear, these were not men anyone was supposed to mourn or pity.

According to the report, the police came into the village with warrants for the arrest of the two brothers, but they resisted arrest and attempted to escape while firing pistols at the police officers. The police fired back, and in the firefight, Jalal Jamalka was shot dead. Kadir Jamalka was injured and taken to a nearby hospital, where he died on the operating table. A police officer suffered light injuries and had already been released from hospital.

I sat back, lowered the paper, ran a hand through my hair and kneaded the muscles at the back of my neck. I took out another cigarette, one which I had rolled myself earlier that morning, filled with the tobacco Ahmed Jamalka had given me. As I inhaled the rich taste of the tobacco I thought of him, some-where across the border, in Syria or Lebanon. Was he following the news from Israel? Was he aware of what had happened to his brothers? Did he realize that these would be the consequences of the revenge he had taken on Rosen?

Around two o'clock I called Sima Vaaknin. I had informed her a few days earlier that Buzaglo was dead and that she could return home. She was supposed to have been back a few hours now.

She told me that Buzaglo's men had trashed her apartment, left many of her clothes in shreds, broke plates and glasses, and used a knife to cut open the sofa.

I went to her apartment to help her clear the mess. It was an unpleasant sight, but we tidied things up quickly, putting all her broken and smashed belongings in the street. Her place looked emptier now, the living room and kitchen barren.

"I'm sorry about all this, Sima. I am responsible. Let me replace what you lost."

"Don't worry about it," she said. "It was time to buy new things anyway, and my vacation was a good one. As for money, I have enough to buy my own things." Our eyes met, and she said, "You know something odd, they didn't touch the bed."

She smiled at me, and I had to work hard to keep from

smiling back. I felt the desire for her course through my body, and the guilt follow closely behind it like a bad aftertaste.

"I don't think so, Sima. It's not a good idea."

She shrugged. "Soon, though. You'll be back here soon."

Toward the end of the day, with the street outside turning darker and colder, I sat with Greta over coffee and told her the whole story, and unlike my talks with Ahmed and Talmon and Reuben, this time I left out no detail, including Sima Vaaknin.

"Do you think she was right?" Greta said.

"Who?"

"Sima Vaaknin, when she said you'd be back to see her soon."

I thought for a moment and then said truthfully, "I don't know. I hope not. I hope I can stay away."

Greta looked at me, and there was sadness in her eyes. "Why? Why hope for such a thing? Because of your guilt?"

"Yes. And because Sima Vaaknin is like a pool of honey—it's sweet and delicious, but you'd drown all the same."

A little later she said, "This police inspector, Rosen, do you think the truth about him will ever come out?"

"No. He'll go down as a hero, someone who gave up his life doing his job, another death in our struggle with the Arabs. That's how he'll be remembered."

"And the rest of them, the three men in Jaffa and the two Arabs in the north, how will they be remembered?"

"They won't," I said. "Like most men, they'll be forgotten by everyone except their families and close friends, and as soon as those people die as well, they'll be remembered by no one."

Which was better than many other people, I thought, the people who had gone into the camps and been turned to dust and ashes, them and their entire families beside them. For them there was no headstone with flowers adorning it. There was no one to say a prayer over them. There was no one to remember their names. They were extinguished and lost and gone.

And perhaps that was why I hoped I would not return to Sima Vaaknin's warm bed—because doing so, I felt, would dull the memory I held of my wife, would weaken the flame of her memory in my mind, the only place in which she was still alive.

## The End

**Thank you for reading *The Dead Sister*.**

Want to read more Adam Lapid?

*The Auschwitz Violinist*, book 3 of the Adam Lapid series, is now available.

**Please review this book!**

Reviews help both authors and readers. If you enjoyed *The Dead Sister*, please leave a review on whatever website you use to buy or review books.

Turn the page for a personal message from the author.

# A NOTE FROM THE AUTHOR

Dear Reader,

Thank you so much for reading *The Dead Sister*. I had a good time writing it, and I hope that you had a good time reading it.

The greatest pleasure I get as a writer is to hear from readers. So drop me an email at contact@jonathandunsky.com with any questions or feedback, or even just to say hi.

Before you go, I'd like to ask you to do a little favor for me. If you had a good time reading *The Dead Sister*, please leave a review on whatever website you use to buy or review books. Good reviews help persuade new readers to give my books a try. I would greatly appreciate it if you'd share your experience of reading this book by leaving your review. Thanks in advance.

Now that that's out of the way, I'd like to tell you a bit about how this story came to be.

I started writing *The Dead Sister* without having a complete plot in mind. I knew who my main character was going to be and I knew that he would be investigating the murder of a young Arab woman—a murder the police, for some reason, were reluctant to investigate vigorously.

What I did not know was everything else. I did not know who the killer would be, nor why the police would not investigate the case properly. I had no clue as to how Adam Lapid would discover who killed Maryam Jamalka.

I started writing that first scene in which Ahmed Jamalka hires Adam Lapid to discover who had murdered his sister, and the book went from there. Each day, I wrote a thousand words or more and slowly but surely, the story began to take shape. Somewhere in the middle of the process, I figured out who the killer would be. I did not know yet how Adam Lapid would figure out the same. So I wrote the ending and slowly filled in the middle. When all was done, of course, I had to tweak the ending quite a bit, but it was in this nonlinear manner that I wrote and finished the novel you just read.

If you enjoyed Adam Lapid's company, I invite you to read *The Auschwitz Violinist*, book 3 in the Adam Lapid series.

If you're a member of a book club and wish to discuss *The Dead Sister*, there are discussion questions right after this author's note.

Thank you again for reading *The Dead Sister*.

All the best,

Jonathan Dunsky.

# BOOK CLUB DISCUSSION
# QUESTIONS

1. What do you think about the changing relationship between Adam Lapid and Ahmed Jamalka? How does the tension between them reflect the larger tensions between Jews and Arabs in the Middle East?
2. Do you see any symbolic meaning to the scars on Adam's back?
3. How would you describe the relationship between Adam and Sima Vaaknin?
4. Both Adam and Sima are victims of severe trauma. What do you think of the different ways in which they deal, or choose not to deal, with their trauma?
5. The setting of Tel Aviv, 1949, is unusual for a detective novel. How well does this setting fit the genre?
6. What were the main themes of this novel?
7. Adam Lapid lost his four sisters in the Holocaust. How does this loss affect his actions and feelings in this novel?

8. Did the solution to the mystery surprise you? If not, how did this affect your enjoyment of the novel?

9. Apart from Adam Lapid, who was your favorite character in the book, and why?

10. In their first encounter, Adam allows Charlie Buzaglo and his henchman, Rafi, to escape with minor injuries. What does this say about Adam's character?

11. Do you think you would have liked living in Tel Aviv, 1949, and why?

12. If you could ask the author a single question about this novel, what would it be?

13. If you could pick a character from the book and have a story written from their point of view, who would it be?

14. Would you recommend this novel to a friend? How would you describe it when you recommended it?

# ABOUT THE AUTHOR

Jonathan Dunsky lives in Israel with his wife and two sons. He enjoys reading, writing, and goofing around with his kids. He began writing in his teens, then took a break for close to twenty years, during which he worked an assortment of jobs. He is the author of the Adam Lapid series and the standalone thriller The Payback Girl.

# BOOKS BY JONATHAN DUNSKY

## ADAM LAPID SERIES

Ten Years Gone

The Dead Sister

The Auschwitz Violinist

A Debt of Death

A Deadly Act

The Auschwitz Detective

A Death in Jerusalem

The Unlucky Woman (short story)

## STANDALONE NOVELS

The Payback Girl

Printed in Great Britain
by Amazon

36191841R00129